SANDRA MARTON

intimate strangers

Harlequin Books

TORONTO • NEW YORK • LONDON
AMSTERDAM • PARIS • SYDNEY • HAMBURG
STOCKHOLM • ATHENS • TOKYO • MILAN

For Lillie, *'petite fleur du bois'*.
If only you were here.

Harlequin Presents first edition April 1988
ISBN 0-373-11067-7

Original hardcover edition published in 1987
by Mills & Boon Limited

CHAPTER ONE

JESSICA HOWARD clutched at the arm rest of her seat. Her white-knuckled grip felt desperate enough to leave fingerprints in the metal frame. If only her heart would stop racing, she thought. If only her stomach would stay put. If only the damned aeroplane were back on the ground.

Two months of rigorous attendance at the Fearful Flyers Club had changed nothing. Well, no, she thought, that wasn't quite true. At least now she could board a plane without looking as if she were going to be ill. To the casual observer, Jessica looked every inch the cool, New York career woman. Only she knew that deep inside herself, Jessie Howard, formerly of Canton, Ohio, looked out at the world firmly convinced that if humans had been meant to fly, they'd have been born with wings.

The big 1011 had barely taken off from New York's Kennedy Airport—and Jessica was half convinced only her silent prayers had enabled it to do that—when they'd hit their first air pocket. Whatever that was. All Jessica knew for certain was that the flight had been like a ride on a roller-coaster. The plane pitched again and she caught her breath. She could never understand people who liked roller-coasters. What they found enjoyable about the tortuously slow climb to the top and the shrieking, headlong plunge towards the earth below baffled her, but at least you could avoid roller-coasters. You couldn't avoid aeroplanes, not if location shots were part of your job.

7

The plane bucked and rolled as if it were a living creature, not a machine made of aluminium and plastic. It was hard not to think of the plane as an animal determined to shake itself free of its human riders ... Jessica had a sudden, vivid image of a cowboy riding a bucking horse at a rodeo. Yes, she thought, that was more like it. If you were lucky, you'd stay on till the end. If you weren't ...

Without thinking, she glanced across the almost empty plane. Well, at least that explained the Marlboro Man, she told herself grimly. There he sat—slouched was more like it—with his eyes closed and that damned relaxed expression on his face. Of course he felt completely at home riding this ... mechanical mustang. He'd probably spent half his life having his bones jarred loose on the back of a horse. Maybe he wasn't happy unless his brain was bouncing around inside his skull. Maybe he thought this was how flying was supposed to be ...

His eyes flickered open and caught hers. She turned away quickly, but not before he'd grinned and nodded at her. There it was again, she thought uncomfortably, that same damned knowing smile, as if he knew how terrifed she was. But he couldn't, no one could. Even the stewardess who'd brought her lunch hadn't suspected a thing.

'We're going to land early,' the girl had said with professional good cheer. 'We've got a terrific tail wind.'

And Jessica had nodded and smiled and waved away the tray of plastic food that made her stomach lurch.

'Nothing for me, thanks,' she'd said, her own smile the equal of the flight attendant's. 'I'm on a diet.'

The girl nodded. 'I understand. Love your outfit, by the way.'

Jessica managed to return the smile. 'Me, too,' she admitted.

Which had been a mistake, of course. A true Manhattanite would have simply smiled and murmured, 'This old thing?' But then, Jessica hadn't quite mastered the rules of the game yet. There were still times she was certain the whole world could see right past her clothes and make-up and know that she was really just little Jessie Howard from Canton, Ohio.

The man had been watching her almost from the minute their plane had left the runway in New York. He had grinned at her then, condescendingly, almost as if he knew she'd been holding her breath while the plane seemed to gather itself together and leap into the sky.

Her glance had drifted away fom him in cold dismissal. The Marlboro Man, she'd dubbed him on the spot, taking in his denim jacket, his faded jeans, his leather boots, his Western hat. Of course he'd think her fear was amusing. He was all teeth, muscle and brawn, a macho stereotype without enough brains to worry about several tons of metal hurtling through the sky in defiance of all the laws of nature. He didn't even have enough sensitivity to understand another person's concern. Well, why would he? Cow punchers weren't very intelligent, she was sure. All they had to do was stay on the top of a horse and yell, 'Yippy ki yay' or something silly like that. Western macho definitely wasn't her style.

The plane had finally levelled off and the 'No Smoking' sign had vanished. She had relaxed and drawn her first easy breath when, suddenly, there he was in the aisle beside her.

'Hi, there,' he'd said in a soft, drawling voice. 'Would you mind if I sat down? We're in for a long flight and ...'

'Yes, I would mind,' she said bluntly. 'I have work to do.'

His smile had been quick and easy. 'I see. Well, if you have a change of heart ...'

'I won't.' She had turned away and lifted her oversized handbag from the floor.

He'd watched as she drew out a crumpled pack of cigarettes and a lighter. 'You shouldn't smoke, you know. It's bad for your health.'

'So is giving advice to strangers,' Jessica said tartly. 'Anyway, aren't you the wrong person to say bad things about cigarettes?'

She couldn't believe she'd said something so stupid even as the words left her lips. But he had chuckled.

'Let me know if you change your mind and want company,' he'd drawled. 'Sometimes the weather gets a little rough over the mountains this time of year.'

Jessica had given him a last cold look. 'Really? How interesting.' And then she'd turned away and stared out the window.

He hadn't spoken to her or even come near her again, but had managed to bother her anyway. Every now and then, she'd had the nagging feeling that he was looking at her and, sure enough, each time she turned around there he was, with that dumb grin on his face. Even now, with the plane dipping and soaring as it defied gravity and the storm that raged outside, he was still watching her and smiling ...

Stop that this very minute, Jessica told herself. There was no storm out there, only clouds and turbulence, whatever that was, at least that was what the pilot had said an eternity ago when he'd asked that his passengers fasten their seat belts and stay in their seats. He'd even made a joke of it. 'We're glad you folks finished lunch before we hit this stuff,' he'd said in a slow Western drawl. 'And we're sure you'll be glad to know that our ETA at Cheyenne is going to be fifteen minutes earlier than scheduled, thanks to these winds.'

Hardly anyone in the half-filled plane had even looked up. They'd all gone right on reading or sleeping—sleeping, for heaven's sake—while she'd glanced around, looking for—well, she wasn't sure what she'd been looking for. Cracks in the plane's walls, maybe, or red warning lights, or . . .

'Miss Howard?'

Startled, Jessica widened her grey eyes and looked up. The flight attendant was standing beside her and smiling.

'I thought you might like some coffee, since you didn't have lunch.'

Jessica shook her head and swallowed audibly. 'No, no, I'm fine, thanks. Er . . . how much longer until we land in Cheyenne?'

'Just a little over an hour. We've made great time, haven't we?'

The plane lurched and the flight attendant swayed with unconscious grace. The girl wasn't even grasping the seat for support, Jessica noticed unhappily. She was the one doing that, and she was sitting down! Deliberately, she let go of the seatback in front of her.

'We certainly have,' she said in a calm voice. 'I have to catch a connecting flight. I was a bit worried about having enough time to make it.'

'Yes, 25B and 53A have connections to make, too.' The flight attendant laughed pleasantly at Jessica's blank look. 'The passengers in seats 25B and 53A, I mean. Both gentlemen are going on to Jackson Hole on Western Air's four o'clock flight. Is that the one you meant?'

Jessica shook her head. Why on earth had she started

this conversation? It was bad enough that she still had another hour to go on board this flying death trap without thinking about the next one.

'No, I'm flying on Wind River Airlines. Will we land near their gate?'

The girl shrugged her shoulders. 'Sorry, I never heard of it. I'm new to this route—I've been flying mostly international. What's your final destination?'

'A place called Eagle Lake,' Jessica said. 'My agency's doing a picture shoot there.'

'I thought so. I told Charlotte—the girl in the rear cabin—I told Charlotte you must be a model. I couldn't help but notice that big bag of yours, just like the kind models carry ...'

'I'm not a model,' Jessica said quickly, trying not to notice that the plane had shuddered hard enough so that the magazine on her lap slid sideways. 'Actually, I'm a fashion co-ordinator for an advertising agency.'

The flight attendant nodded. 'No wonder you've got such great taste in clothes.'

Jessica looked up at the girl and smiled. 'It also explains how I can afford them,' she said. 'I get a fantastic discount.'

'The girl laughed. 'Lucky you. Well, let me know if you change your mind and want something, OK?'

Jessica nodded her head and smiled faintly. She watched as the flight attendant sauntered casually up the aisle, trying to imagine what it was like to earn your living by flying, day after day, week after week ...

She sighed and leaned back in her seat. You did what you had to do, she thought. She was a living testament to that. Two years ago she'd come to New York ready to become the world's greatest photographer. Who'd have dreamed she would end up making her living by preparing models for somebody else to photograph? Not that hers wasn't a good job—she met interesting people at the Allen Agency and she went to unusual places, even if she did have to fly to get to most of them. It was just that she seemed to have got further and further from the career she had dreamed of since her mother had bought her a simple snapshot camera for her twelfth birthday.

The plane dipped and Jessica glanced at her watch. Only another hour and they'd be landing. At least they were flying more steadily now. The seat belt sign was still on, but every now and then some determined soul made his or her way down the aisle towards the lavatories at the rear of the plane. They all walked with the care and precision of people who have had too much to drink, but, as far as Jessica could tell, they all made it. Surely she could manage it, too? It would be nice to splash some cold water on her face. And it was probably time to run a comb through her hair and put on some fresh lipstick. After all, there might be someone from the Macello Fur account catching the same connecting flight at the Wind River Airline gate. She might not be the only one joining the group at Eagle Lake Lodge at the last minute.

With exaggerated care, Jessica unbuckled her belt and rose to her feet. She turned and grasped the top of the seat behind her. So far, so good. There was hardly any sensation of motion at all; the plane seemed to be flying smoothly and steadily for a change. Still, she touched each seat as she moved slowly down the aisle, breathing a sigh of relief when she reached the first lavatory. It was unoccupied, and she opened the door and stepped inside.

The mirror above the tiny sink confirmed her suspicions. Her hair certainly did need combing, she thought, rummaging in her handbag. It was a tumbled mass of dark, glossy curls. And she needed more than lipstick; her face was so pale that her eyes looked like

dark grey pools against her skin. She needed some
blusher and maybe a light dusting of powder. Her glance
slid to her leather vest and matching pants. The flight
attendant had been right; it was a good-looking outfit. It
just wasn't very comfortable. An old pair of cords and a
sweatshirt would have made more sense, especially once
she reached Eagle Lake Lodge and started crawling
around behind the camera, fluffing curls and soothing
egos. But clients wanted a certain image. Jessica
understood that; the only trouble was, Jessie didn't, and
sometimes, when she looked in the mirror, it was Jessie
who looked back at her, Jessie who shook her head
sorrowfully, remembering a time when the only images
that mattered were the ones you saw through a
viewfinder . . .

Jessica tossed her head and took a deep breath. Her
outfit was going to be perfect for a place like Eagle Lake
Lodge, a place that would add just the right touch of
rugged glamour to the new client's image. It would be an
interesting few days, she thought, living on a dude ranch
in the West. Not that they'd really be roughing it, of
course. Her boss would never let reality go that far.

A sudden image of the man in the plane flashed into
her thoughts. He certainly had the look of reality about
him. She was certain no designer had fitted him for those
jeans or that jacket. In fact, when he'd stood beside her,
she'd almost expected to smell hay and horses . . . Jessica
laughed softly. Actually, what she'd smelled was a
combination of leather and something spicy and clean. It
had been rather pleasant, when you came right down to
it. She'd only registered those things on a professional
level, of course. If you worked for an advertising agency,
it was natural to notice when somebody had modelling
potential. And she had to admit the man was good-
looking in a rough, outdoorsy way. Not just his face, but

his body. When he'd stood beside her, she had had to tilt her head back to see his face, he was so tall. And he had broad shoulders and a narrow waist and ...

With a suddenness that sent her stomach into orbit, the plane lurched violently.

'Oh, God,' she moaned, clutching desperately at the sink. The plane bounced again, and she turned and pushed open the door. All she could think of was getting back to the fragile security of her seat and her seatbelt. 'Excuse me,' she murmured, trying to pass a woman blocking the aisle. 'Excuse me,' she repeated, a bit more loudly. 'I have to get back to my seat.'

The woman turned and smiled brightly. Jessica recognised the face of the flight attendant.

'Sorry, Miss Howard, but we've started serving our final snack. I'm afraid you'll have to go round the other way,' she added, gesturing to the serving cart completely blocking the aisle. 'Just up the other side and across in front of the bulkhead.'

The plane dipped and the floor seemed to sway under Jessica's feet. 'Yes, all right,' she said in a whisper. 'That's fine.'

Carefully, she manoeuvred her way to the far aisle. How could they serve anything when the plane was bouncing like this? How could her fellow passengers be so unconcerned? People were dozing and reading and drinking coffee and talking to each other as if they weren't travelling in this ... this flying eggshell.

'Ohhh ...' The empty word was torn from her throat as she stumbled sideways. Something had hit the plane, she was sure of it, or they had hit something. A wall, maybe, or another plane, or ...

'Are you OK, ma'am? Did you hurt yourself?'

A pair of strong arms closed around her. For the span

of a heartbeat, Jessica leaned into their security and strength.

'What happened?' she whispered. 'Have we hit something?'

The arms tightened around her and the man chuckled softly. 'It sure felt that way, didn't it? But you don't have to worry, ma'am. That was just an air pocket.'

That soft drawl ... And that clean, outdoorsy scent ... Lord, it was the cowboy. She caught her lower lip between her teeth and pulled free of the stranger's arms.

'Thanks for your help,' she said carefully, forcing her eyes to meet his. 'I'm sorry I disturbed you.'

He grinned and shook his head. 'No problem, ma'am. I wasn't doing much of anything, anyway.'

There it was again, that damned smile ... 'No, I can see that,' she said frostily. 'If you'll just let me by ...'

'It's a long way back to your seat, ma'am. And it's gotten a bit bumpy. Why don't you settle down next to me for a while?' His smile broadened as his eyes raked over her. 'I'd be glad to have some company. Especially such pretty company.'

'I'm not interested,' Jessica said in a chilled voice. 'I thought I made that clear hours ago.'

He laughed softly. 'You certainly did, ma'am. The other thing you made clear was that flying scares the daylights out of you.'

'It doesn't,' she said quickly, feeling the rush of colour to her cheeks. His eyes narrowed and she thought of the way she'd clutched at him only seconds before. 'I ... I just don't particularly like flying in this kind of weather,' she added defensively.

'The weather's fine,' he said pleasantly. 'It's the air turbulence. I tried to tell you about the mountains and the thermals they kick up in the fall.'

The plane seemed to dip into a trough and Jessica

blanched. 'Look, I really don't need a lesson in physics.'

'It's just simple aerodynamics and meterology.'

'All I need is to get back to my seat. If you'd just step aside . . .'

The stranger nodded. 'If that's what you want. But you're going to have to go back the way you came, ma'am. That serving cart's moved while we were talking and it's blocking the way to your seat, if you counted on heading that way.'

Jessica shot a desperate look across the cabin. He was right. The flight attendant had moved the cart up the aisle. She would have to go back the way she'd come, down that endless aisle and across the next, and then all the way up again . . . The floor tilted suddenly, and the man's arm slid around her waist.

'You really could get hurt standing in the aisle like that,' he said. 'Why don't you sit down next to me? Lots of people are afraid of flying,' he said quietly. 'It's nothing to be ashamed of.'

'I'm not af . . .' The plane dipped again and her legs turned to rubber. 'Well, maybe I'll sit down for a second,' she said carefully, as she let him guide her into the seat beside him. She closed her eyes with relief as her bottom touched the solid surface. 'I . . . I guess it's more sensible to stay put,' she said in a low voice. 'I mean, what's the point of going back to my own seat now?'

The man leaned across her, his lean fingers fumbling for her seat belt. 'Absolutely,' he said solemnly.

She swallowed as the plane rolled heavily. 'After all,' she said in a thready whisper, 'we'll be landing soon.'

He nodded his head as the belt snapped shut. 'Right,' he said. She glanced down as his hand accidentally brushed against hers. His fingers were calloused and hardened, but his touch was strangely gentle. Unaccountably, she felt the colour rise to her cheeks.

'So I might as well stay here and . . .' The plane dipped and rose like a cork in the ocean and Jessica's face paled.

'You're fine now,' he said quietly. 'And there's nothing to worry about.'

Suddenly, it seemed pointless to lie anymore. 'I wish I could be sure of that,' she blurted.

'You can be. I told you, this is fairly normal turbulence. And this airline has a fine safety record.'

'Really?' She laughed nervously. 'I wish I'd known all that a couple of hours ago.'

'You would have, if you'd been willing to listen to me. I knew you were terrified—that's why I offered to sit with you.'

She glanced at him, prepared for the condescending smile she'd seen on his face before. And he was smiling— even his hazel eyes were smiling—but suddenly Jessica realised there wasn't anything condescending about it. He was smiling at her the way you'd smile at a child about to take its first step alone. He was trying to reassure her and tell her she'd make it. A feeling of shame washed over her.

'I . . . I guess I owe you an apology,' she said in a small voice. 'I didn't think my fear showed.'

'It didn't, not unless you know the signs. But I've seen white-knuckled flyers before. And for someone like me, someone who loves flying, it's hard not to offer a hand.'

Jessica nodded. 'I feel awful. I thought you—well, I thought you were . . .'

The man grinned crookedly. 'Yeah, I know what you thought. And you weren't entirely wrong, you know. I've got to admit, the possibility of soothing the frazzled nerves of a pretty woman had its appeal.'

His answer was so blunt that she had no choice but to return his smile. There were worse things than sitting here talking to somebody as good-looking as this, she thought. And she had to admit that he'd taken her mind off flying. It really had been foolish to have given him the brush-off before. The flight would have been much pleasanter with him as a seatmate. He seemed like a nice enough man even if she couldn't picture him in a three-piece suit, or even walking along a city street. And he really was awfully good-looking in a virile sort of way. Those hazel eyes and that straight nose and that thick, dark hair that he kept raking off his forehead ...

'Do you fly this route often?' she asked.

He shook his head. 'Nope.'

'You don't? But I thought ...'

'I simply fly a lot. After a while, you can tell what's normal about a flight from what's dangerous. I could tell you thought the plane was going to fall apart, so ...'

'I didn't' she said defensively, and then she shrugged her shoulders. 'Well, maybe I did.' A faint smile tugged at the corners of her mouth. 'The thing is, I don't really believe that things as heavy as this plane can fly. Sometimes I'm half convinced they only do because all the passengers believe they can. You know, like Wendy and Peter Pan. If enough of them stopped believing, down it would go!'

He laughed with delight. 'That's a new one on me. Somebody once told me he was always tired after a flight because it took a lot of energy to keep flapping his arms so that the plane would stay up.'

Jessica smiled. She could feel the tight knot of fear that had been inside her unravelling. It was comfortable back in this section of the cabin. The seats around them were all vacant; the window shade was pulled down, lending a pleasantly shadowed atmosphere to the area where they sat. She could almost relax.

The seat felt as if a giant hand had tilted it under her. At the same instant, the lights dipped and dimmed.

Without conscious thought, Jessica clutched at the stranger's arm.

'What's happening?' she said sharply, 'What was that?'

'It's just more turbulence,' he said quickly. 'That's all it is.'

The plane bounced sharply and Jessica's fingers tightened on his arm. 'It's more than that,' she said. 'The lights . . .'

'They'll come back on in a second or two. Take it easy.'

'Something's wrong, I know it,' she insisted, turning towards him. 'There is, isn't there?'

Her eyes were so dark, so round with fear, he thought. She reminded him of a frightened doe he'd once found along a trail in the Cascade Mountains. The animal had got caught in some damned fool's snare and it had been too terrified to work its way free. It had been as much a captive of its own fear as of the ropes that had caught it. The girl beside him was the same. She was past explanations, past listening. And the damned plane really was bucking and bouncing. He thought again of the deer, of how he'd wished to hell there were a way to distract it while he worked at setting it free . . .

'Just think about something else,' he said softly, leaning towards her. 'Think about Cheyenne, Have you been there before?' She shook her head. 'It's a nice town,' he said, covering her hand with his. 'Do you like mountains? There are some beautiful ones outside the city. Are you on vacation?' She shook her head again. 'Business? So am I. I . . .' The plane seemed to drop violently. He knew what was happening; there were cross winds buffeting them. They were feeling the effects of wind shear; she had good reason to be afraid, not that he'd ever admit it to her, but he could read the terror in her eyes. 'Think about something else,' he repeated inanely.

'I can't,' she whispered. 'I can't, I can't ...'

Weeks later, when he tried to figure out how it had all happened, he would wonder what made him reach out and pull her into his arms. He told himself it was all he could think of to distract her, that there just didn't seem to be any other way, but it still wasn't an adequate explanation for why he suddenly wanted to hold her against his heart and kiss the fear away from those huge grey eyes. Whatever the reason, he knew he'd never forget that first soft touch of her mouth against his.

Jessica felt his hands bite into her shoulders. She was so fixated on the conviction that these were her last moments of life that it took a couple of seconds before she realised what he was doing. By the time his arms slid around her and his lips found hers, it was far too late to stop him from kissing her with a low, sweet thoroughness that seemed to demand a response. She struggled against him for a surprised, angry instant and then the warmth of his arms and the taste of his mouth drove everything else from her mind. Her eyelids closed and her head fell back against the seat as her lips parted beneath his. She was free of fear, free of everything but a kaleidoscopic wonder at what was happening ...

'Ladies and gentlemen, we're sorry for the rough ride, but we know you'll be glad to hear that it's all smooth sailing ahead. We'll be landing in Cheyenne in about fifteen minutes. Please make sure your seats are in an upright position and that all lap trays are folded.'

The captain's impersonal voice hit her like a slap of cold water. With a gasp, Jessica wrenched herself free of the stranger's embrace. In one quick motion, she unlatched her seat belt and got to her feet.

'You're really some piece of work,' she said in an

angry hiss. 'I had your number right the first time, after all.'

For once, she noticed with grim pleasure, the man's ready smile failed him. He rose to his feet quickly, an expression of such confusion on his handsome face that she wanted to cheer. It was scant comfort to think that he was unused to having women walk away from him, but it was better than nothing.

'Better luck in Cheyenne,' she said coldly. 'I'm sure your act will wow 'em in cow country.'

'Please, wait,' he began, but she turned on her heel and marched up the aisle. At least, the plane was co-operating. It didn't twist or dip or even tilt all the way back to her seat. She sat down just as the 'No Smoking, Fasten Seat-belt' sign flashed on. They'd be landing in just a couple of minutes, thank heaven. The Marlboro Man wouldn't have a chance to bother her again. All she had to worry about now was her connecting flight on Wind River Airlines. And somehow, that seemed easier to deal with than what had just happened.

CHAPTER TWO

JESSICA tapped her foot impatiently as she waited beside the empty luggage carrier belt at Cheyenne Airport. The graffiti scrawled on a nearby post summed it up perfectly: Next time, it said, before the flight, I've got to remember to travel light. There was a real truth there, she thought. If she'd packed everything in a suitcase small enough to take on board with her, she wouldn't be standing here, wasting precious time while her luggage made the trip from the belly of the 1011 to the terminal. And she wouldn't be doing her damnedest to avoid the man from the plane, either. She hadn't seen him since they'd landed, but she had the definite feeling he was lurking somewhere. Well, she thought grimly, if he was and if he so much as said one word to her, just one word, she'd do what she should have done on the plane and slap his face silly.

The luggage belt lurched into life and the first suitcase from the New York flight appeared. And, thank goodness, there was hers, just behind it. Jessica grunted as she heaved the battered bag from the moving belt. It had been with her since her last year of high school when the senior class had gone on a trip to Washington, DC, but it had never been quite this heavy before, stuffed as it was with clothes and her hair dryer and last-minute things she thought the models might need. And there were cameras, of course, carefully wrapped inside layers of clothing. It was a good thing the suitcase had wheels, even though the wheels seemed to have a life and purpose of their own, because there wasn't a trolley in sight. Jessica sighed and began to tug the unwieldy baggage after her.

'Excuse me . . .' She paused beside a security guard. 'Could you tell me where to find Wind River Airlines?'

'The man shrugged his shoulders. 'No idea.'

'Yes, but . . .'

'Try the Information Desk,' he said. 'Through that door.'

Jessica nodded. 'Thanks.'

The suitcase bounced along behind her. Every now and then it seemed to change direction and steer itself directly towards whatever obstacle was nearest. By the time she had gone through the door, her arm had begun to ache. She breathed a sigh of relief when she finally saw the Information Desk against the far wall. Carefully, she navigated the suitcase through a small crowd, murmuring 'excuse mes' and 'sorrys' as she went, hoping the occasional bumps and thuds she heard weren't the sounds of the little wheels running across anybody's feet. She waited at the counter until the clerk turned towards her.

'I'm looking for the Wind River gate.'

The woman's smile was blinding. 'Yes?'

'I don't know where it is,' Jessica said patiently.

'Oh, I see. Well, I'm afraid I don't, either.'

The toothy smile was still radiant. Jessica ran her tongue over her lips.

'Do you think you could find out, please? I have to make a flight there in . . .' She glanced at her watch and frowned. '. . . in less than fifteen minutes. I don't want to miss it.'

The woman nodded. 'Of course,' she said pleasantly pulling a book towards her. 'Just give me a minute—here it is. Just follow those green signs for WestAir. You won't have any problem finding it.'

'But it's Wind River ...'

'You want the WestAir gate, miss. The green signs.'

'Ah. I see.' Jessica smiled her thanks and stepped away from the counter, dragging the suitcase along after her. Well, at least things were looking up. She'd heard of WestAir—it was a large airline that flew in the western United States. Either the receptionist back at Allen Associates had got the name wrong or Wind River shared facilities with WestAir. Not that it mattered. All that mattered was getting there on time.

Automatically, she began walking faster, glancing every now and then at the green WestAir signs. The suitcase behind her wobbled dangerously and headed towards the wall. Jessica swallowed a muttered obscenity and dragged it into line. She had passed through another doorway; a long corridor loomed ahead of her. She quickened her pace, tugging sharply at the suitcase as it changed direction once more. There was a faint dragging sensation against her hand and then the suitcase ground to stop. She almost stumbled at the intensity with which it seemed to work itself into the floor. Jessica brushed a lock of hair out of her eyes and knelt down.

'Damn!' she said softly. Two of the wheels lay behind the suitcase, belly up like little dead animals. She touched her finger to them and then scooped them into the palm of her hand. Now what, she thought, rising to her feet and looking up and down the corridor. There wasn't a trolley in sight. In fact, there was no one in sight. The corridor was lined with flight gates, but all the waiting areas around them were dark. But the little green signs for WestAir still pointed the way. Jessica took a deep breath and grasped the leather handle of the suitcase with both hands, groaning as she hoisted it up from the floor.

'Come on, Jessie, you can do it,' she muttered under her breath.

She'd survived two weeks of aerobic dance classes, hadn't she? And a month of early-morning jogging through Central Park. And a trial membership at that health club ... Oh boy, she thought, oh boy, if she'd only stuck with one of those things long enough to make it count. Each time, she'd wanted to work off a couple of pounds, not grow muscles. And she needed muscles right now, she knew. The handle was digging into her palm—actually it felt as if it were gouging a hole in the tender flesh. But that wasn't as bad as the pain shooting up her arms and shoulders and back ...

'Hey ... Excuse me. Sir?' Jessica tottered towards a man carrying a mop and pail. He was stoop shoulderd and sparse white hair lay across his shiny scalp, but he was the most beautiful sight she'd seen all day. He put down his pail as she approached. 'Is there a porter around?' The man shook his head. 'Well, is there a way for me to call for one?'

'Nope. That suitcase of yours broken?'

Jessica nodded. 'Yes,' she said, 'yes, it is ...'

The old man shrugged. 'Don't make things the way they used to,' he said, bending towards the pail. Jessica held out her hand.

'Wait, please. Can you at lest tell me how far it is to the Wind River gate?' He looked blank and she shook her head. 'WestAir,' she said. 'How far is it to WestAir, then?'

'Gotta say what you mean,' he said laconically. 'Westair's just down the hall a piece. Not far.'

'Not far,' she repeated, staring at the endless corridor ahead. With a sigh, she lifted the suitcase again. 'Thanks.'

So much for Western hospitality, she thought,

marching onward. Or was it Southern hospitality? No
matter. Whichever it was, it wasn't anything to boast
about. New Yorkers were supposed to be cold and
impersonal, but at least at Kennedy Airport they had
trolleys and luggage carts and people! This place was the
wide open West, all right. Miles and miles of airport and
not a soul in sight. And the ones who were certainly
weren't very helpful. Oh, they sounded friendly enough,
but that was just because there was a kind of softness to
their speech, like that man on the plane.

Jessica's shoulders stiffened. That had been some
welcome to the West, hadn't it? Imagine that ... that
cowboy thinking he could take advantage of her! Was
she supposed to have fallen into his arms and welcomed
his advances? She blushed hotly, remembering the way
she'd melted into his arms after the first shock of
surprise. Well, of course she'd melted. She'd been scared
half to death. He'd been relying on that, hadn't he? A
clear image of him flashed through her mind. The broad
shoulders, the rakish smile, the firm chin ...

Why would a man like that have to rely on anything
but his own good looks? Not that she liked the type, she
thought hastily, wincing as the suitcase bounced against
her leg. Behind that 'aw, shucks, ma'am' exterior lurked
the instincts of a tom-cat, which explained why he'd
zeroed in on her fright. It made her an easy target.
But he'd seemed so sensitive, so caring when he talked
to her ...

'Dear God, Jessie, all that bouncing in that plane must
have scrambled your brains,' she said aloud.

She paused and let the suitcase drop to the floor. It
couldn't be much further now. For one thing, she was
going to run out of corridor, soon. The end of it was just
ahead. But there were still WestAir signs on the wall
every now and then. In fact, she noticed with a surge of

hope, wasn't that one coming up larger than the others?
Yes, yes it was, and it pointed to the left. With a sudden
resurgence of energy. Jessica lifted the suitcase and
started to walk quickly towards the green sign.

'Thank goodness,' she whispered. There it was, in
small print down at the bottom of the sign. Wind River
Charters, Charters? She'd flown a charter flight once, to
Ohio, to visit her parents. It had been a regular 727 and
they'd served lunch and drinks and she'd survived,
which was really all that counted.

Her footsteps slowed and she frowned. The green sign
had said all the right things, but she was in the wrong
place. She had to be. There was a waiting area, all right,
with chairs and tables, but the place was dark and empty.
The flight gate was closed; it, too, was deserted. But
there was nowhere else to go. The corridor ended here.
There was nothing but an exit door. Suddenly, Jessica's
breath caught in her throat. Had she missed her plane?
That had to be the answer. Yes, she was late—five
minutes late. The plane wouldn't have waited for her.
What now? She could picture the models, photographer, light man, make-up man, and the Macello
Fur people all standing around at Eagle Lake, waiting
for her, waiting while a six-figure account went down
the tubes because she hadn't been able to find a trolley
when she needed one ...

'Wind River? Are you the passenger for Wind River?'

Jessica jumped at the sound of a human voice. 'Yes, I
am,' she said, smiling hesitantly at the man who'd
pushed open the flight gate door.

He wiped his hands on his overalls and nodded. 'They
said you might be looking for the right gate.' He jerked
his thumb over his shoulder. 'It's just outside, ma'am.
Through here.'

'Well,' Jessica said brightly, trying not to groan as she

lifted her suitcase again, 'that's good to hear. I'd about given up hope ... It was nice of them to hold the plane for me. I'm sorry I'm late, but ...'

Her explanation tapered off into silence as the man edged into the corrdor and let the door swing shut behind her. She blinked in the sudden daylight; she'd expected to find herself on the boarding ramp leading to the plane, not on the airfield. In fact, there was no plane. Well, she thought, looking around her in confusion, that wasn't entirely true. There *were* planes, lots of them, but they were all little ones, the kind that had always made her think of Charles Lindbergh or the Red Baron. There certainly wasn't a real plane anywhere in sight. She turned back to the door and tried to open it, but it seemed to have locked automatically.

She sighed and dropped her suitcase to the ground. So, she thought unhappily. She'd missed her connecting flight after all. Either they'd taxied away only a few minutes ago or the mechanic had a bad sense of humour. Not that it mattered; what mattered was getting to Eagle Lake Lodge. There had to be a bus or train or a car she could rent. But she couldn't face the thought of dragging that damned suitcase another inch. If she could just leave it here and arrange to have a porter pick it up ...

A flicker of movement alongside one of the planes caught her eye. Jessica peered across the field. Was there ... yes, there was someone there, a man, doing something or other to the plane, cleaning it or fixing it ... She lifted the suitcase and hurried towards him. Maybe she could leave the thing with him for a few minutes. Of course, if he was half as helpful as the mechanic or the maintenance man she'd spoken to, he wouldn't let her, but there was a chance. Maybe if she offered him a tip ...

The man's back was to her. Jessica cleared her throat
and took a deep breath.

'Hello,' she called, as loudly as she could, but there
was no answer. It occurred to her that she could hardly
expect one; the field was alive with the noise of large
planes landing and taking off. She sighed and trudged
towards him. Her suitcase felt as if it weighed a ton, and
her feet hurt. Her stiletto heeled boots had looked terrific
when she bought them but they weren't really made for
walking endless miles of airport corridors. Well, the
worst was over. She'd arrive late at the Lodge, but she'd
get there before they began shooting tomorrow. It was
true, she was a day late to begin with, but that wasn't her
fault. She was replacing Marla Anderson, who had got
sick an hour before the agency had flown everybody out
of New York yesterday morning. It wasn't even her fault
that she'd missed this connecting flight, either. Just as
soon as she got this mechanic to agree to watch her
luggage, she'd find out about renting a car or whatever . . .

The man was out of sight, behind the plane. She
dropped her suitcase for the last time and sat down on it
wearily. Her eyes flickered idly over the plane while she
waited for him to reappear. It was blue and white and
she couldn't help but think it looked a little like one of
the wind-up toys you saw kids playing with in Central
Park. She grinned; she almost expected it to have a
rubber band instead of a propeller, but it had a propeller,
all right, although it was in a funny place, not in the
plane's nose but on top of it, and facing backwards.
Jessica shook her head. There was no accounting for
tastes. It was a weird-looking little plane; even more
weird was the thought that anyone would be willing to
fly inside something so strange and insubstantial. Not
that she would tell that to the mechanic or the owner or

whoever they guy was who was coming around the plane, of course. The last thing she wanted to do was to insult the man.

She got to her feet and smiled brightly. 'Hi there. Nice day, isn't it?'

He straightened up and looked over at her. She couldn't see his face; he was wearing one of those Western hats and huge sunglasses, but she'd caught his attention. He wiped his hands on his overalls and watched her.

'Look, I wonder if I might ask a favour of you,' she said quickly, walking slowly towards him. 'I—er—I was supposed to catch a four o'clock flight here. On a Wind River plane?' Why on earth had her voice drifted upwards like that; she sounded like a nervous kid. She cleared her throat and smiled again. 'The thing is, I missed the flight and I broke the wheels on my suitcase and . . . If you'd just let me leave it here, I'd be very grateful. I'll get a porter to pick it up.'

The man shook his head.

'No?' she said. 'You mean, I can't do that?'

'Sorry,' he said.

'I'll only be gone a few minutes. Look, it's important to me . . .' Jessica blinked and tilted her head to the side. There had been something familiar about his voice, something she'd heard before. But then, everybody sounded the same in this place. They all drawled and . . . No, she thought staring at him. No . . .

He was unzipping his greasy overalls; underneath, he wore a demin jacket and jeans. 'Hi,' he said pleasantly, pulling off his sunglasses. 'What a nice surprise.'

Jessica closed her eyes and moaned softly. After a second, she opened them again. The man from the plane was still there, smiling at her. In fact, he was moving towards her.

'I had no idea you were . . .'

'I'll just bet you didn't,' Jessica said quickly. 'Don't bother coming any closer. What did you do, follow me?'

His smile broadened. 'You seem to have followed me. I was here first, in case you hadn't noticed.'

'Never mind all that,' she answered, brushing aside the logic of his remark. 'I'm going into the terminal. Don't you get any ideas.'

'You can't,' he called, as she hurried towards the door. 'It's locked, Miss Howard.'

She stopped half-way there and took a deep breath. Of course it was locked. Well, she thought grimly, then she'd walk across the airfield. There were people off in the distance. She'd have to pick her way among the planes taxiing back and forth, but it was better than staying here. Anything was better than that.

'How did you know my name?' she demanded. 'Did you ask the flight attendant? She shouldn't give out personal information. I . . .'

The man came up behind her and reached for her suitcase. 'She didn't,' he said, while they silently grappled for possession of the handle. He won easily, taking the heavy case away from her as if it were empty. 'Actually, I only just figured out that you must be Jessie Howard.'

'Jessica,' she said immediately.

'Jessica,' he repeated with a grin. He started towards the little blue and white plane and she had no choice but to hurry after him.

'Wait a second,' she gasped, her heels clicking loudly on the asphalt. 'What are you doing with my luggage?'

It was such a senseless question; she could see what he was doing with it. He was tossing it into the toy plane.

'I'm loading it on board,' he said reasonably.

'You can't do that,' she sputtered, and he grinned again.

'Sure I can,' he drawled. 'Relax, Jessica Howard. You haven't missed your connecting flight to Eagle Lake.'

'I haven't?' He shook his head and she looked all around her. 'But I must have. I don't see a Wind River aeroplane . . .'

Her words whispered into silence as she blinked. The man nodded his head and ran his hand along the little blue and white plane's fuselage. How had she missed it? she wondered dumbly. There, neatly printed beneath its identification numbers, were the words WIND RIVER CHARTERS.

'No,' she murmured, backing slowly away from the toy plane, 'no, it can't be.'

He nodded again. 'I'm afraid it is,' he said quietly, and his teeth flashed whitely in a quick grin. 'And that's not even the worst of it, Jessie.'

'You mean . . .'

This time, he chuckled aloud. 'You're a fast one, Jess,' he said, 'Yup, that's right. I'm your pilot.'

CHAPTER THREE

THE first thought that came into her head was that there was a hidden television camera nearby. Perhaps she was the subject of one of those awful programmes that depend on the embarrassment of people caught unawares in set-up situations. But it was a desperate thought and she discarded it as soon as it surfaced. A practical joke, then. But she knew no one who went in for such grim humour; besides, you needed an audience for a practical joke, didn't you? And, even in the panic of the moment, she knew that not even this ... this range-riding Romeo standing in front of her would go to all this trouble just to be alone with her. She refused even to consider the possibility that this really was her connecting flight to Eagle Lake. Her mind veered away from such an awful thought without any conscious effort at all. That meant it had to be a mistake. Of course it was a mistake, she thought with relief. After all, she'd seen the models and the cameraman and the others fly off in a regular plane, a real plane, just yesterday.

'There's been some sort of mix-up,' she said calmly. 'I'm with the Allen Agency.' The cowboy nodded and smiled. 'In New York,' she added, and he nodded again. Was he completely dense? 'I'm not going camping or hunting or fishing or wherever it is people go when they rent little things like your plane ...'

'It's not mine,' he said politely, patting the fuselage. 'I work for Wind River. I guess I'm working for your agency, too, come to think of it. And I know where you're going; a buddy of mine flew your people there yesterday afternoon.'

'What do you mean, you work for the agency, too?' she asked suspiciously.

'I'm the guy who's going to be your firm's air taxi for the next week. The location you people picked is pretty isolated.'

'What were you doing in New York?'

He flashed her another of those toothy grins. 'It's a long story. I was meeting with some people on business when I got a hurry-up call from Wind River. My buddy was going to be your agency's delivery boy until somebody in your office suddenly decided they wanted a guy who was knowledgeable about Eagle Lake.'

'Knowledgeable?'

'Yeah, familiar with its wildlife and plants and ... why are you looking at me like that?'

'Which is it?' she asked suspiciously. 'Did they hire you to fly a plane or identify plants?'

He grinned and pushed his hat back on his head. 'I swear, Jessie ...'

'Jessica,' she said again.

'I swear, I'm a qualified pilot. And I know you don't like to fly.'

Her mouth opened and shut again. There was no point in denying the truth of that, she thought, not when she'd made a fool of herself in front of him less than an hour ago. She looked from him to the plane. What she had to make him understand was that he was trying to over-simplify things.

'It's not the flying,' she said carefully. 'You see, I don't like your plane.'

He turned and looked at the plane as if he'd never seen it before. 'Why not?'

'Well,' she said, 'it's too small.' Did I really say something as dumb as that? she thought. But the man simply nodded his head.

'It is small, I agree. But it's a good plane.'

'Oh, I'm sure it is, but . . .'

'And it'll get you where you have to go,' he said reasonably. 'To Eagle Lake. That is where you want to go, isn't it?'

Jessica nodded. 'Yes, but I don't have to fly there,' she said with a sudden sense of relief. 'I can rent a car.'

'There aren't any roads to the Lodge, Jessica.'

She tilted her head to one side. 'No roads?' she replied slowly. 'Come on, don't be silly. This place is in the Tetons, not the mountains of the moon.'

'There aren't any roads,' he repeated patiently. 'Some eccentric millionare built himself a house in the thirties and that's the way he wanted it. The only way to get in and out is by air. How come you don't know any of this? Don't they tell you people what kind of assignments they're sending you on?'

'It was a last-minute thing,' she said quickly. 'I was busy on another job when this was set up . . . Look, what about a boat? I know there's a lake.'

'We can't get there by boat, not unless you want to paddle a canoe up river and across three lakes.'

'But . . .'

'Look, Jessica, this is a tough little plane and it'll get us there quickly and safely.' He paused, aware suddenly of the changing slant of the sun and the developing clouds. 'We're just wasting time,' he said, turning towards the plane.

'I'm not sure . . .'

'Fine,' he said brusquely. 'I'll tell them you aren't coming.'

My God, she thought, the man had no heart! For a minute or two, she'd thought she had glimpsed the man who'd soothed her on the 1011, but now she realised he had just been jollying her along, doing and saying whatever it took to get her on that ridiculous plane. And why wouldn't he? He'd been hired to ferry in supplies and that's what she was. On the plane from New York, she'd been a diversion. Now, she was a sack of something to be delivered. But she was neither; she was a woman with a job to do. She squared her shoulders and stared past him at the plane. It had no steps or ramp.

She took a step forward. 'How do I get into your sardine tin?' she asked in a steady voice.

He grinned and held his hand out to her again. 'It's easy.'

It hadn't been easy, of course, she thought a short while later as she sat rigidly beside him in the cockpit of the little blue and white plane. He had tugged and pulled and hoisted her on board in ways that were as ungraceful as they were immodest, but she was past caring. All that mattered was keeping her stomach and her nerves under control while he buckled her in—her fingers were too numb with fear—and hoping her teeth wouldn't chatter while he turned on the engine and adjusted a million controls and dials and put on his headset and spoke to the control tower. Finally he smiled at her and said, 'Here we go, Jessie,' and she was too terrified even to remind him her name was Jessica.

She closed her eyes as soon as they taxied towards the runway. They paused for only a little while. She heard him say something to her and suddenly they were rushing down the runway, gaining speed, moving faster and faster and then she knew by the thump of wheels being retracted into the fuselage that they'd left the ground and were in the air.

'We're up, Jessie. Why don't you open your eyes and take a look?'

'Soon,' she said carefully, not wanting to explain that it would take her a while to work up the courage. She could feel the faint sensation of motion, but it wasn't the bone-jarring ride she'd feared. The engine wasn't as loud as she'd anticipated, either, although she could hear it, thank goodness. She swallowed hard. 'How high are we?'

'High enough for the view to be terrific.'

She swallowed again. Then with cautious slowness, she raised her eyelids and stared straight ahead.

'Hi, there,' he said cheerfully. 'How're you doing?'

Jessica turned her head slowly and looked at him. 'Do you have a name?' she asked finally.

He grinned. 'Chad,' he said, extending a hand to her, 'Chad O'Bryan.'

'Please, please, put your hand back on the wheel.'

'It's a control yoke. And it's OK ...'

'Please, Mr O'Bryan. It makes me nervous to see you let go of it.'

'Considering how well we know each other, Jessie, I think you ought to call me by my first name.'

She glanced at him again, a quick blush rising to her cheeks, but he was looking straight ahead with no discernible expression on his face. She thought of their sudden, passionate embrace in the 1011 and the way his hands had touched her when he'd helped her board a few minutes ago and her blush deepened.

'How much longer until we get there, Mr O'Bryan?'

She put a deliberate emphasis on the name, pleased to see that his mouth hardened as she said it.

'Not very long, Miss Howard. Just sit back and relax.' He shifted his weight and a smile flickered across his mouth. 'If you can, that is.'

She decided there was no point in answering. In a few minutes, they'd touch down at the Lodge—she wouldn't dwell on the landing just yet—and she'd be among her own friends. Well, not friends. Fellow workers. Well, no, not that either. The models were nice girls, but they lived a life all their own, never seeming to eat or drink or go out at night for fear of gaining a pound or a wrinkle. And the director was a nice guy but he and the light man seemed to have something going between them ... Jessica sighed. That left Hans, the photographer, and he'd been cold as ice since the time he'd returned the stills she'd asked him to look at. It had taken her weeks to work up the courage.

'Your photos could use better processing,' he'd sniffed.

'Yes, but are they any good?'

'Not bad,' he'd said, turning on his heel and walking off.

The way he'd said it had told her nothing. No matter; she was still a long way from landing a job as a photographer or even an assistant. But she could learn a lot about taking pictures just by watching the pros who shot photos for Allen Associates. Not that she was really interested in fashion photography; she'd always wanted to do portraits and human interest stuff, but the lighting and techniques were the same.

'The Tetons,' Chad said. 'Just below us.' She nodded her head. 'Take a look,' he urged. 'They're really something to see.'

She swallowed and turned towards the window, waiting for the first cold clutch of fear to grasp her. Until now, she'd carefully avoided looking anywhere but straight ahead at the sky and clouds. Keeping her thoughts on everything but the fact that she was hanging up here above the earth in this toy.

They were flying over a rolling landscape of rounded brown and green mountains. They looked almost close enough to touch under the soft light of the late afternoon sun. She could almost feel the power and isolation of the slopes below. And they were travelling slowly enough so that there was time to enjoy the play of light and shadow. It occurred to her that the scene below would make a spectacular photo . . . Cautiously, Jessica raised her eyes and looked out of the windscreen. Was the sky always this blue? There was a depth to the colour she'd never noticed. And the clouds . . . They were like surrealistic wisps of froth stretched across a sapphire sea.

'Pretty, isn't it?'

She nodded. 'Yes, yes, it is,' she said, a tinge of surprise in her voice. 'This is different from the way things look in a real plane.'

Chad grinned. 'This is a real plane, Jessica. More real, in a way, than those commercial jobs. This is what flying is all about. It's . . .'

'Look,' she said suddenly, leaning towards him, 'I never knew birds flew this high!'

'That's a pair of golden eagles, I think. This is migration time, and this is one of their routes.' He watched as she moved her head carefully to the side and then he grinned. 'You can get out of your seat and look at them from the window, if you like.'

'Stand, you mean?' She shook her head. 'No, thanks. This thing is barely big enough to sit in.'

'It's big enough to hold that piece of furniture you were dragging around. What have you got in that thing? Scrap iron?'

It was impossible not to return his smile. 'Clothing,' she said. She laughed at his arched eyebrows. 'Well, equipment, too.'

'I thought my buddy took a load of equipment out yesterday in the big plane.'

'I'm sure he did. This is my own stuff.'

'What did you say you were? The co-ordinator?'

Jessica nodded. 'Fashion co-ordinator. I'm responsible for what the models wear and who does their make-up and hair.' He looked as if she were speaking in tongues, she thought, and she sighed. 'It's hard to explain.'

'And they pay you for doing that?'

It was hard not to laugh aloud. That was the same question she sometimes asked herself, particularly after she'd spent the day reassuring a size six model that she did not have a tummy bulge or walked her feet off trying to locate the perfect prop for a photo only to find it had been cropped out of the picture later on.

'Yes,' she said, 'they do, indeed.'

Chad nodded. 'Do people really notice that kind of thing? Make-up and hair-styles, I mean?'

Jessica's eyebrows arched. Well, after all, she thought, what could you expect from a cowboy? For all she knew, he even slept in his boots and jeans.

'All the time,' she said.

'Yeah, but ...'

'Fashion is a multi-million-dollar business. It employs a lot of people. This layout we're doing at Eagle Lake, for instance ...'

Jessica glanced at the man beside her and sighed. Here she was, giving her best 'fashion is not frivolous' speech, the one she'd given herself when she first got this job, and he wasn't even listening. He was peering out of the window towards some white clouds that seemed to be boiling up from the ground. She frowned as she stared at his face. It was taut with concentration and something else. Worry? Concern? She felt a sudden knot in the pit of her stomach.

'Is something wrong?' He shook his head, but he didn't answer. She watched as he picked up his headset and slipped it on. 'Mr O'Bryan, please answer me. Something's the matter, I can tell. I ...'

'Just be quiet for a minute, Jessica. Nothing's wrong. I just want to check something out with Area Control.'

She listened while he spoke to something he called Cheyenne Routing. There couldn't be anything wrong, she thought, not when he sounded so calm and matter of fact. He identified their aircraft and destination and then he asked some questions about the weather. Not all of it made sense to her, but the gist of it seemed to be that the strange-looking clouds were storm clouds and he wanted to know more about them. Jessica ran her tongue across her lips. She could feel the plane rock, ever so slightly, and she reached out and touched her fingertips to the panel in front of her. The plane rocked gently again.

'Mr O'Bryan ... Chad? Is ... is everything OK?'

'Sure,' he said, but it seemed to her that his normally husky voice was tense. 'I just want to be sure I don't ride us through any rain.' He flashed a quick grin in her direction. 'I want to give you a smooth, easy flight, Jess.'

She nodded her head, her eyes riveted to his hands. He was fiddling with the dials and doing things with the wheel—the yoke, she reminded herself—and his feet were moving, too. She knew those pedals beneath his feet were called rudders. She had no idea how they worked, but it didn't matter. All that counted was that the plane was turning, slowly but steadily, away from the clouds. When his concentration lessened, she breathed a sigh of relief.

'Are we all right?' she asked in a small voice.

Chad nodded. 'Yeah, we're fine. I knew there was some bad weather coming, but it's moved faster than anybody expected.' He glanced at her and smiled reassuringly. 'Don't worry, Jessie. All that's happened is that we're going to take a little longer to get to the lodge.

I've altered course a bit ...'

The plane lurched to the side. 'What was that?' she asked.

'I told you, there's some weather out there. We're going to hit a couple of bumps for a minute or two while I go around these clouds ...'

Chad broke of as the plane lurched again. He had pulled his headset down around his neck and now she heard a loud burst of static from the earphones.

'There's some electrical interference. It's from those thunderheads. That's what those clouds are called,' he said, as if he'd anticipated her next question. 'It'll take a while for me to try and go around them.' He looked at her and then back at the windshield. 'Just keep your seatbelt buckled and take it easy.'

Of course she'd take it easy, she thought. Of course she would. She wouldn't even ask him why he'd try to go around the thunderheads even though that was not quite as positive as what he'd said at first.

Think about something else, she told herself, remembering what she'd learned at the Fearless Flyers. Think about something positive, like the great pictures you're to take whenever you have some time off during the next few days.

Suddenly, the thunderheads were all around them. Jessica glanced at Chad, waiting for him to offer an explanation, but he said nothing. Finally, she cleared her throat.

'I ... Er, I thought you said we were going to go around these clouds.'

'Yeah, well, I'm trying.' His voice was tense, almost curt.

'Can't we go above them?'

'Not unless you don't need to breathe oxygen. Clouds like these go up thousands of feet.' He pulled the headset on and spoke into the microphone.

'Why do you keep repeating everything? Isn't anybody answering you?'

'Look, do me a favour and keep quiet, OK?' he growled without looking at her. 'Just for a few minutes.'

'I thought this was going to be smooth and easy,' Jessica said. She heard the faint edge in her words and she took a deep breath. 'If you'd just tell me what's going on ...'

'Be quiet,' he said sharply. 'I'm trying to hear.' He frowned and then pulled the headset off. 'Damn,' he muttered. 'Nothing but static.'

They were flying deep within the thunderclouds now and the sky outside the cabin windows was thick charcoal fog. Drops of moisture lay like translucent beads on the glass. The plane was shuddering violently like a dog shaking its coat free of rain. Jessica closed her eyes as bolts of lightning lit the sky. It would all be over soon, she told herself. In just a little while, they'd touch down on Eagle Lake and she'd smile and turn to Chad O'Bryan and make some kind of little joke about his idea of what constituted an easy flight and ...

She caught her breath as the wind buffeted them suddenly; just as suddenly, it eased off. Like a cat playing with a mouse, she thought. Like a cat letting the tiny, frightened creature think it could get away from its deadly power ...

Think about what a great story this will make, she told herself, twining her hands in her lap. Think about talking about this once you're back in New York. They'll love it. The guys at the office ... The plane dipped and slammed downwards as if it had fallen in a trough. Jessica ran her tongue across her lips. She wanted to say something—anything—but her mouth wasn't going to obey her. Suddenly, Chad's hand covered hers.

'You'll be OK,' he said. 'I won't let anything happen, Jess. I promise.'

Her eyes widened and met his. 'Are we going to crash?'

He shook his head, but his face was white with tension. 'No,' he said grimly, 'we're not going to crash. I'm going to get us out of this. You'll see. We ...'

Jessica's indrawn breath caught in her throat as the plane suddenly flipped over. For endless seconds, they hung upside down in their seats and then, as if a giant hand had snatched them up, the plane righted itself again. There was a loud banging sound on the roof, exactly is if the same hand had decided to pound its way into the cabin.

'It's the storm,' Chad yelled, his voice almost lost above the sudden noise of rain and hail pelting against the thin metal skin of their aircraft. 'If we can just ride it out for another few minutes ...'

She nodded her head, so amazed that the plane was still intact that she couldn't trust herself to speak. A tough little plane, Chad had called it, and that's what it was, all right. Boy, she thought suddenly, when they got out of this, she'd never be afraid of flying again. This was—what was it called when you were forced to confront your phobia face to face? Aversion therapy, that was it. Some people paid a fortune for it, and here she was, getting it free ...

The same giant hand snatched them up again. She was ready for it this time; her fingers dug into the arm of her seat while the little plane was buffeted from side to side. She had a sudden, crazy image of someone shaking a pair of dice and then they were tossed free.

'Are you all right?' Chad yelled. She nodded again

and he flashed her a grin. 'That's the girl,' he said. 'Just hang on. I think the worst is over ...'

A blinding flash of light zigzagged through the sky before them. Jessica gasped and drew back in her seat.

'My God,' she whispered. 'Wasn't that awfully close?'

'Don't worry. It ...'

The lightning struck again with blinding force, lighting the cabin and scenting it with ozone. Jessica's brows drew together; something had changed.

'Chad?' she said.

He shook his head and stared at his instruments. Her glance followed his; she saw the spinning needles and dials and knew they were incapable of telling him anything. She bit her lip, watching while he fumbled with the switches on the dash, and then, suddenly, she knew what was different in the little cabin. It was the silence, the overwhelming silence ...

'The engine ...?' Her voice was a faint whisper at first, and then it gathered strength. 'Chad, the engine ...'

His hand closed tightly over hers. 'Listen to me, Jessica,' he said clearly. 'We're going down.'

She wanted to tell him he was wrong, to accuse him of playing a bad joke, but the sighing of the wind and the downward tilt of the little plane insisted that he was telling her the truth. 'Call the airport on your radio,' she said. 'They'll help us.'

'The radio doesn't work. Anyway, they couldn't help us.' His hand closed tightly over hers. 'Are you listening, Jess?'

Her eyes swept his face and then went to the windscreen. Strange, she thought calmly, but the weather seemed to have eased. The clouds were still there, but the hail that had been pelting the plane had ceased. 'I heard you,' she said finally. 'You said we were going to crash.'

His fingers bit into her flesh. 'No, I did not, damn it! I said we were going down. There's a difference. I can get us down safely—we can do a deadstick landing on that lake just ahead ... I want you to do exactly as I say, Jessie.'

She swallowed drily, watching as the trees came up to meet them. The tops of a tall stand of firs seemed close enough to touch. Beyond, she could see the wind-tossed water on the lake.

'Is that lake big enough to land on?' she whispered.

Chad's lips pulled back from his teeth in a mirthless grin. 'It better be. We haven't got a hell of a lot to say about it any more.' He squeezed her hand one last time and then he took a deep breath. 'OK, Jessie,' he said, 'put your head down on your lap and link your hands behind your neck.'

How could it take this long to die? she thought. How could everything suddenly happen in slow motion?

'Put your head down,' he said sharply. 'Damn it, Jessie ...'

'But ... but what about you?'

'Just do as I tell you.'

The lake was just ahead of them, gleaming dully through a narrow gap in the trees. God, she thought, it's such a small lake. It's only a pond ...

'Get down,' he roared. His hand was heavy on the back of her head as he forced her head down. 'Everything's going to be all right.'

Calmness enveloped her and she wanted to tell him not to worry, that she was fine and that she'd do exactly as he'd instructed. But everything was happening too quickly. The plane was going down or the water was rushing up to meet it, she wasn't quite sure which it was.

There was a heavy slap and then they were skimming along the lake at a speed she couldn't believe and the shoreline was just ahead and the trees were leaning in on either side . . . Her ears rang with the unexpected shriek of protesting metal. The plane seemed to hit a wall, but that was impossible, she thought clearly, because there was no wall.

The last thing she was aware of was sudden, absolute silence as blackness exploded all around her.

CHAPTER FOUR

'JESSICA ... Come on, Jessica. Open your eyes.'

Jessica stirred and sighed. Someone was calling her name. The voice was a persistent buzz, forcing her back from the clouded edged of sleep, rising above the soft slap of the waves. Her head hurt. It always did when she'd had too much sun at the beach and that was where she was now, wasn't it? She was at the beach; she must be, and she must be lying on a float out in the water, being rocked gently from side to side ...

'Look at me, Jess. Open your eyes.'

She wanted to do as the voice asked. For one thing, once she opened her eyes she could swim to shore and get out of the sun. Maybe then this awful headache would go away. But she was tired. Her eyelids were heavy. It was so much easier to fall back into the swirling darkness.

'Look at me,' the voice insisted.

It took all her power of concentration, but finally she forced her eyes open. Her glance flickered over her surroundings and she frowned.

'What happened?' she murmured in a faint voice. She cleared her throat and focused on the face swimming before her. Gold-flecked, hazel eyes peered into hers. The cowboy, she thought groggily. What's he doing at the beach with me?

'Welcome back,' he said softly. 'You had me worried for a minute.'

'Chad?' She frowned, and then panic flooded through her as reality returned. 'My God, we crashed, didn't we? Didn't we?' she repeated, trying to get to her feet.

49

His hands pressed lightly but firmly against her shoulders. 'Take it easy,' he said quickly. 'We're fine, Jessie. We're down and we're safe. I just want to check your forehead.' She flinched as he bent towards her but his touch was surprisingly gentle. 'Here,' he said, pulling off his neckerchief and holding it out to her, 'wet this with your tongue.' Obediently, like a child who'd hurt her knee at the playground, she did as he asked. 'It's just a superficial cut,' he said, dabbing at it carefully. 'We'll do a better cleaning job later. This'll do for now.' He leaned back and held up his hand. 'How many fingers do you see?'

'Two,' she said, wincing slightly.

He nodded. 'Good. OK, Jess, let's get going. We haven't got all that much time.'

'Get going?' A peculiar kind of lethargy seemed to grip her, and she sat quietly while he unbuckled her seat belt. 'Where?'

'To shore. We're in the middle of a lake.'

She glanced out the window, noting, almost with surprise, the grey water surrounding them, tossing the little plane from side to side.

'I don't remember anything,' she whispered.

'You must have whacked your head on the instrument panel. We touched down OK, but there was one hell of a surprise waiting for us.'

'I ... I don't understand ...'

Chad edged past her and knelt behind her seat. 'I didn't see the rock shelf we're wedged on until it was too late. It ripped the hell out of the hull. I don't know how long it'll be before water starts pouring in.'

'There's water in here already,' she said slowly, for the first time noticing the inch or so that covered the cabin floor. 'Hey, that's my suitcase,' she added quickly. 'What are you doing?' It was a stupid question, she thought. She could see precisely what he was doing—he was slashing through the soft-sided case with a small pocket knife he'd pulled from his jeans. 'You didn't have to do that,' she said. 'You could have asked me for the key ...'

She broke off in mid-sentence as he raised his eyes to hers. She watched in silence as he finished slicing the suitcase open and then she fumbled at the buckle of her seatbelt.

'My cameras,' she said, stumbling out of her seat as he began rummaging through her clothing. 'Give me my ...' The plane lurched slightly at the shifting weight and Chad caught her hand in his.

'Don't make any sudden moves, Jessie. We want the plane to stay afloat as long a possible.'

'What?' She swallowed hard and her eyes widened. 'You mean we're sinking?'

He nodded his head and turned back to her suitcase. 'I'm afraid so. Have you got any warm clothing in here? Things made of silk or wool?'

She stared past him through the cracked windscreen. Grey waves rose ahead of them; beyond the nose of the plane lay a thick bank of fog.

'But ... how will we get to shore?' she asked in bewilderment. 'I can't even see it from here.'

'Catch these things, will you?' Chad asked. Obediently, she turned to him and he tossed articles of her clothing into her arms. 'You can't see the shore because of the rain. But we'll be OK; amphibians carry dinghies.' He nodded over his shoulder and she looked towards the windscreen again. This time, she spotted a smudge of yellow visible outside the plane. 'I inflated it as soon as we were down.' He leaned forward and dug into the corner of the suitcase. 'I found your cameras,' he said. 'Sorry.'

Jessica peered over his shoulder at the broken bits of plastic and glass. Three months worth of paychecks, she thought with a sigh, but the tilting floor and the water lapping at her boots seemed to minimise the sense of loss.

'Have you got some jeans in here? And shoes . . .'

The plane lurched again, and she bent and touched Chad's shoulder, 'Shouldn't we—shouldn't we be getting out of here?'

He nodded. 'In a minute. But we're going to need warm clothing. It's wet and cold out there.'

The thought of what awaited them outside the plane sent a shudder through her. She pushed the thought aside and squatted down beside him.

'I have these sweaters,' she said. Plucking them from the suitcase. 'And this blouse is silk. Is that the kind of thing you mean?'

'Yeah, that's fine. And at least you've got a pair of sneakers,' he added, pulling out her old running shoes. 'Put on the sweater and then get those boots off and put the sneakers on instead.'

'Listen,' she said quickly. 'Why don't we get to shore first and then I'll change my clothing? I really don't think we ought to take the time right now . . .'

'And I don't want you tearing holes in the dinghy,' he said flatly, as he rose to his feet and hunched his way forward.

Well, she thought, she wouldn't argue with that. She certainly didn't want any holes in the dinghy, either. It looked fragile enough, bobbing and dipping under the wing. Quickly, she pulled off her boots and laced up her sneakers. Then she moved cautiously forward. The plane swayed, almost delicately, from side to side and the water licked at her feet.

'Now what?' she asked, hoping he couldn't hear the terrified drumming of her heart.

'Now we get the hell out of here.' He pulled a canvas backpack from under his seat and stuffed her few pieces of clothing into it. 'OK,' he added, wrenching open the door. 'Let's go.'

She started to take his outstretched hand and then she saw her shoulder-bag lying on the seat. 'Wait,' she said 'just let me ...' There was a groaning sound and the plane lurched sideways. Water began to pour in from under the rudder pedals.

'Hurry, Jessie ...'

She snatched up the bag and moved towards the open doorway. Chad tossed the pack into the dinghy and then eased himelf out after it. The dinghy was so small ... He held his hand out to her but she hesitated, watching as the little craft bobbed dangerously under his weight.

'Come on, Jess, we haven't got much time.'

She wanted to do as he asked, but her feet felt as if they'd been nailed to the cabin floor. There was a gurgling sound behind her and the plane tilted sharply to the right.

'Don't be afraid,' he said quietly. 'Just give me your hand ... That's it,' he said soothingly as she reached towards him. Her fingers were ice-cold with fear, and he brushed aside the realisation that she had no way of knowing that what lay ahead of them was probably going to be even rougher. 'Lean towards me, Jessie. I won't let anything happen to you. I promise.'

Jessica held her breath and leaned towards Chad's upstretched arms. The plane and the dinghy were both bobbing and tossing in the stormy water, one going up as the other went down. His arms closed tightly around her and she closed her eyes as he lifted her into the dinghy.

'Now, get down and stay still,' he ordered.

Stay still? She fought back a sudden insane desire to laugh as she hunched lower in the tiny craft. She was afaid to breathe, much less move. She felt completely vulnerable and at the mercy of the lake, the rain, the wind, the groaning, creaking plane ... She glanced at Chad as he freed the line that tied them to the wing. She'd felt safe for the few seconds he'd held her in his arms while he helped her into the dinghy. She'd felt the same way in the 1011 flying out here, she thought suddenly. Well, sure she had. When you were scared, human contact made all the difference.

She gasped as the dinghy lurched wildly. Chad had pushed off from the plane and begun rowing towards the shoreline dimly visible behind them. The rain had eased off to a cold drizzle. The lake and the sky were the colour of old pewter, with the sky's ominous greyness offset by the lake's windlashed waves.

Jessica shivered and burrowed into the wool sweater Chad had made her put on. Cold spray blew in her face and she wiped it away with a trembling hand. If only she could see the sun again ... Suddenly, it occurred to her that the sky's leaden look was not only because of the clouds and rain. It was late; the sun would be setting soon. Their plane had crashed and they were in the middle of a storm-tossed lake and darkness was coming on. A sense of total weariness overtook her. What was the point, she thought, closing her eyes. They'd never make shore; if the storm had been powerful enough to bring down a plane, what would it do to this fragile piece of rubber?

'Jessie? Jessica!' Chad's voice sliced into her like a whip. She lifted her head and looked at him blankly. 'I need your help,' he said. 'I can't make it to shore alone.'

She frowned and stared at him uncomprehendingly. Finally, she shook her head. 'I ... I can't help you,' she whispered. 'There's nothing I can do. I ...'

'Yes, there is, Jessie,' he said firmly. 'You can direct

me to that clear place there—do you see it? That rocky
ledge . . . just concentrate on getting us there.' His eyes
flickered over her pale face but she said nothing. Chad
drew in the oars and laid them along the gunwales. 'Of
course,' he said without inflection, 'if that's too
difficult, we can sit out here until dawn and watch the
plane go under. It's up to you.'

It was as if the lake had been waiting for him to stop
paddling. Wind-whipped, white-frothed waves
snatched at the little craft and began to pull it away from
the shore. Jessica clutched at the dinghy's sides and
stared at him.

'You have to give me directions, Jess,' he said, raising
his voice over the keening of the wind. 'There's not
much point in my rowing if I don't know where I'm
going.'

Anger flooded through her. Was he going to let the
water bounce them around like a cork? She peered past
him, expecting to see nothing but grey sky and water.

'The shoreline,' she said in surprise. 'I can see it!'

Chad nodded. 'Can you see the ledge?'

A weight seemed to lift from her chest. She shifted to
her knees and nodded her head. 'Yes—to the left, Chad.
That's it, yes, good, good. Straight now—we're almost
there.'

He dug the oars into the water and they surged ahead.
'You see? I told you I needed you to tell me where we
were going.'

Jessica bit back the desire to tell him he hadn't known
where he was going when he was piloting the plane,
either. If he had, they wouldn't have ended up inside
those clouds . . . 'I'm a good pilot,' he'd said. Well, she
thought, watching the rapid approach of the rocky
shore, at least he was a good oarsman.

'Slow down,' she yelled. 'There are rocks coming up!'

The dinghy lurched and bumped against something. The shore, she thought, sighing with relief. They'd made it, and there was still some daylight left. Plenty of time to walk to the nearest road and flag down a car, unless they were near the lodge. Now that she thought about it, they probably were. What a wonderful thought—a little hike up a trail and then a hot bath and a rum toddy and ...

She scrambled to her feet as Chad hopped into the shallows. Clutching her shoulder-bag, she stepped gingerly ashore, wincing as the cold water soaked through her leather pants. Almost immediately, she felt the chill against her flesh and she shivered.

'Catch!'

She glanced up just in time to see Chad's pack sailing towards her. She caught it in mid-air, staggering under its surprising weight, then watched as he secured the line from the dinghy to a sapling growing among the rocks.

'OK,' he said, taking the pack from her, 'let's find a more sheltered spot than this and then we'll get you warmed up.' He peered towards a rise to their left and slung the pack on his shoulders. 'There's a stand of birches up there. Let's try them.'

Jessica fell into line behind him. She hoisted her heavy bag over her shoulder and tried to match his stride.

'How far is the lodge from here?' she asked.

'I'm not sure.'

'We were flying long enough so that it can't be very far.'

He glanced over his shoulder at her. 'That bag's probably slowing you down. Why don't you leave it?'

'Leave it?' She looked from him to the bag and shook her head. 'All my things are in it,' she said. 'My credit cards and my wallet and my cheque book ...'

Chad started to say something and then he nodded. 'Right. Well, try and keep up with me, Jessie.'

'That's just what I'm doing,' she puffed. 'But it would be easier if you slowed down.'

'It'll be dark soon, Jessie. I want to get to the top of that ridge before that.'

Her breath whistled in her lungs. 'Can we find the lodge in the dark?'

There was a brief silence. 'No,' he said finally.

She waited for him to say something more but he didn't. 'Well, then, how about the nearest road?' she wheezed. 'Is it very far?'

'You'll get your wind back faster if you don't talk.'

She started to answer and then she closed her mouth and nodded. He was right. She was breathing so hard it hurt.

'We're almost there,' he called a few minutes later. 'Are you cold?'

No, she thought, not cold. Freezing. 'A little,' she said. 'But . . .'

'When we get to the top of the ridge, you can change out of those wet things, those trousers, especially.'

'But the road . . .'

'Save your breath, Jessie. We can talk in a few minutes.'

'Yes, but . . .' Her lungs felt as if they were on fire. 'OK,' she panted, putting her head down and plodding after him. He was right. There would be time for questions when they got to the top of the hill. Right now, all she had the strength to do was concentrate on putting one foot in front of the other. Left, right, left, right . . . Almost there. And then she could sit down and take a deep breath and let her heartbeat return to normal. Her leather trousers were making it harder to climb the grade. They were not just wet but unpleasantly constricting. It would be nice to swap them for her jeans—after she got her breath back. Until she managed that, she wouldn't be able to do anything . . .

'Whoops,' she gasped, stumbling into Chad's back, 'sorry. I didn't realise you'd stopped.'

They were in a small clearing surrounded by birch trees. The trees blocked most of the wind. The rain had stopped completely and a pale sun shone weakly on the horizon. Jessica sighed with relief and leaned back against one of the trees.

'That's better,' she said breathlessly. 'That hill was steeper than I . . .'

'Here,' he said, tossing her a sweater and an unfamilair pair of jeans. 'Get out of those wet things while I get a fire going. There's bound to be some dry kindling under these trees.'

'In a minute,' she panted. 'Let me recover first.'

'Now,' he said.

Jessica's eyebrows rose. 'I just want to get my bre . . .'

He put his backpack on a boulder and began to rummage through it. 'Don't give me excuses, OK? Just do as you're told.'

'Do as I'm told?' she repeated dumbly. He couldn't have said that . . .

'That's what I said. Change your trousers.'

Count to ten, she told herself. This man just saved your life. Take a deep breath and count to ten. After a bit, she looked down at the jeans he'd given her.

'These aren't mine,' she said. He looked up and she held the trousers out to him. 'These must be yours. Mine are pale blue . . .'

'You're right. Those are mine. Just get them on. Believe me, you don't need to co-ordinate fashion out here.'

A tightness was forming in her chest. 'I wasn't

thinking of fashion,' she said slowly. 'It's just that my own jeans would fit me better . . .'

'Right,' he said digging ino his pack again.

She waited for him to say something more, but he didn't. The tightness was spreading to her stomach.

'Then why don't you give them to me? I know you took them with us. I saw you take them out of my suitcase . . .'

He raised his head and looked at her. 'We're going to get along much better if you do what I tell you, Jessie.'

'Mr O'Bryan,' she said through her teeth, 'I know this isn't the time to argue about it, but I think I should tell you I don't much like your attitude . . .'

'Just be a good girl and go change your jeans. You look like a drowned rat.'

'I am not a girl,' she said with dignity. 'I am a woman.'

'And a damned stubborn one.'

'No, I'm not. Each time I ask you a question, you ignore it, Or you bark out orders. I . . .'

He got to his feet and put his hands on his hips. 'You asked me if we could reach the lodge before dark and I said we couldn't. You asked me if I knew how far the nearest road was and I said I didn't. You said you didn't like the colour of my jeans . . .'

His eyes were flashing and his chin jutted forward, but she stood her ground. Don't let him intimidate you, Jessie, she told herself. That's what he's trying to do.

'I said,' she repeated with exaggerated care, 'that your jeans would be too big for me . . .'

'Forgive me,' he said sarcastically. 'That's right. You were afraid my jeans wouldn't fit you right . . .'

'I don't particularly care how they fit,' she said, her voice rising. 'It just doesn't make much sense to wear something three sizes too big when I have my own.'

'My jeans are made out of denim,' he said. 'Yours are light cotton. Mine will be a lot warmer. Satisfied?'

The tightness began to ease from her chest. 'Yes,' she said. 'All you had to do in the first place was give me a reason.'

'The only reason you need is that I told you to do it.'

Back to square one, she thought in disbelief. Let it go, Jessie, an inner voice said. But suddenly she remembered his arrogance on the flight from New York and then her mind skipped to the unknown hours stretching ahead. Establish the ground rules now, Jessie, another voice said, and she lifted her chin.

'Perhaps we should sort things out a bit, Mr O'Bryan. I'm grateful that you got us down safely . . .'

'You're welcome.'

'But we're not on a ship. You are not the captain and I don't have to obey your orders.'

'If you want to get to a road, that's exactly what you'll do, Miss Howard. We haven't got the time to argue over everything I say.'

'I wasn't arguing with you, for heaven's sake, I was simply asking something . . .'

'And I gave you an answer. Just do what I tell you and we'll get along fine. Is that simple enough?'

She threw her hands in the air. 'What it is, is simple-minded,' she said, tossing caution to the wind. 'But I'm in no position to argue, am I? You're the expert. You're the one who nows which way the road is, not me.' She turned away on her heel and then she spun towards him again. 'Or am I assuming too much?'

Even in the fading light, she could see him recoil. 'And what is that supposed to mean?'

'I think it was pretty clear.'

'If that was supposed to be a crack about my flying ability . . .'

'Would you mind going somewhere while I change my clothes?'

'Listen, Miss Howard, my flying ability is the only reason you're alive and in one piece.'

'In one piece? Is that why the plane is in the lake and we're here?'

'It's a damned good thing the plane isn't here,' he said, gesturing at the growth of trees that surrounded them.

'It's just too bad it isn't where it's supposed to be. Eagle Lake, for instance.'

'Is this your professional opinion? I didn't know you had a pilot's licence.'

'I probably have as much right to one as you do,' she said. 'I'm not the one who flew us into a storm. I'm not the one who landed on the rocks. I'm not the one who ...'

'Right, you're not. You're just the one who was so damned scared of doing what millions of other people do every day that you needed a nursemaid. If I hadn't had to spend so much time holding your hand and cajoling you ...'

'Oh, just listen to you! Holding my hand and cajoling me. Right! Was that what you were thinking about when you should have been thinking about that storm? "Ah won't let anythin' happen to you, Jessie,"' she mimicked cruelly. 'What's the matter, Mr O'Bryan? Did you think I'd fall into your arms with gratitude if you got me to Eagle Lake in one piece?'

Chad snorted in disgust. 'Just what I needed—a tenderfoot who's read one romance too many. My God, lady, you must think you're the world's most irresistible female. Listen, I'd just as soon have a ... a Barbie doll in my bed as you. At least they don't talk.'

Her smile had all the warmth of a shark's. 'Is that

what you got used to during those long nights riding the range? How cute.'

For an instant, she thought she'd gone too far. His eyes narrowed and he took a deep breath. She stood her ground and waited; finally, he turned way from her.

'I'm going to start a fire,' he said tonelessly. 'Do whatever you please about those wet trousers. I don't really give a damn.'

Jessica watched as he stalked off into the trees, her chest rising and falling rapidly. 'Who does he think he is?' she muttered as he vanished from view. 'From the minute I laid eyes on that man, I knew what he was. He ...' She looked at the jeans he'd given her and made a face. She'd told him she'd put the damned things on, but that wasn't enough. What did he want? Was she supposed to click her heels and salute?

She stepped behind a bush and peeled off her wet leather trousers. It was a relief to get out of them. His jeans were much too large, as she'd expected, but they were, indeed, warm. She rolled them to ankle length, pulled the belt from her own trousers, and looped it through the jeans. Then she pulled off her damp sweater and changed it for the dry one. She felt better almost immediately. Her socks were wet, but not unbearably. Anyway, she could dry them by the fire he was going to build. She ran her fingers through her hair, and stepped into the clearing.

The final rays of the sinking sun lit the lake dully. Jessica searched the wind-ruffled water and then swallowed drily. All traces of the plane had vanished; it was as if it had never existed. Her thoughts flashed back to the minutes before the crash—she could almost hear Chad's voice reassuring her, talking her into calm acceptance of what lay ahead.

She sat down on the boulder and shifted uneasily. No

matter how you looked at it, he was the reason they were still alive. Anger had made her say things she knew were untrue. It wasn't his fault they'd crashed—you didn't need a degree in engineering to know that a bolt of lightning had probably been the culprit. He'd made what had seemed to her to be an impossible landing on a dot of water and then he'd got them out of a sinking plane; and she'd said thank you for all that by insulting him in every way possible, starting with his flying ability and ending with his masculinity.

Not that he hadn't asked for it—all that stuff about following orders and blind obedience had made her see red, but she could tolerate it for the time it took to get her out of here. If he wanted to make like Daniel Boone for a while, let him. She owed him that much.

She got to her feet. He wasn't back yet. Well, when he returned, she'd apologise for the things she'd said. For now, she would do something useful and show him that she took all this seriously. They needed kindling, he'd said. OK, she thought, bending and picking up some small branches, she'd collect some. After all, she'd been a Girl Scout, hadn't she? She smiled as she picked up another piece of wood. This is for you, Troop 126 of Canton, Ohio, she thought.

It was no wonder Chad had gone into the woods after kindling. There was precious little in the clearing. She narrowed her eyes and stared down at the ground. There was a piece, and there was another ... She bent and picked up the wood, her eyes searching for more. There was some as she reached the first trees; she nodded and began to collect pieces in earnest. Yes, there were lots here, enough so she could be choosy.

She had an armful of wood when she heard Chad's voice calling her. She looked up in surprise. How could he sound so far away? And how could it have gotten dark so quickly? There was a thick greyness all around her. She could barely see beyond the nearest tree. She felt her pulse leap into her throat. Time to get back to the clearing.

But where was the clearing? She turned in a circle, widening her eyes as if by doing so she might force light from the darkening sky. But she could see little and what was visible had no meaning. Every tree looked like every other; where was the path?

'Jessie?'

Chad was calling her again, She could hear his voice more clearly this time. 'I'm here,' she yelled. 'Chad?'

'Where are you, Jessie?'

'Here,' she called ... Where? she thought helplessly. 'Chad?' She stumbled over a tree root. 'Where are you?'

'I'm coming, Jessie,' he called. 'Just stand still and talk to me so I can locate you.'

'I—I—what do you want me to say?'

'Louder, Jessie. I can't hear you.'

She closed her eyes, trying to ignore the dark shadows that seemed to have sprung up everywhere. A chill ran through her and she took a deep breath.

'I said—I said I'm sorry I said those things to you before,' she called into the darkness. 'I—I was just angry ...'

'Louder,' he called again. 'Louder, Jessie.'

She took a deep breath. 'I'm sorry for the things I said,' she yelled. 'You saved my life today—twice. Maybe even three times,' she said more softly, swallowing hard as she stared nervously over her shoulder into the blackness of the forest. 'Will you forgive me, please? You're really a good pilot, Chad. I know that the crash wasn't your fault ...' Her words stumbled to a halt and silence embraced her. 'Chad?' she said in a breathy whisper. 'Can you hear me?'

'No,' he said. 'You'll have to repeat it again.'

'I said . . .' Jessica caught her lip between her teeth. He had materialised from the shadows—he was standing in front of her. 'That's not fair,' she whispered. 'You heard me the first time.'

'Damned right,' he said, and she could hear the laughter in his voice. 'But you owe me, Jessica Howard.' He reached towards her and took her hand in his. 'How the hell did you get all the way out here?'

'I was collecting firewood . . .'

Chad sighed. 'A rule of survival, Jessie. There are three things you have to know: where you've been, where you are, and where you're going.'

'I *was* in the middle of nowhere. I *am* in the middle of nowhere, and I was trying to *return* to the middle of nowhere,' she said with a forced smile. 'I guess that's not quite the rule you had in mind.'

'You're shivering,' he said, putting his arm around her. 'Come on back to the clearing and I'll build a fire.'

'Yes, that's a good idea.' Her teeth chattered together. 'Isn't that foolish? It's not that cold . . .' Her voice broke; suddenly, there were tears in her eyes. 'I—I'm sorry,' she whispered. 'I don't know what's wrong with me.'

Chad's arm tightened around her. 'Nothing's wrong with you,' he said gruffly. 'It's me. First, I scared the life out of you by riding you through the worst storm I've ever seen and then I almost killed you in a crash landing and now here I am, marching you up a mountain without even asking you if you were OK, or if your head still hurt, or if you were scared . . .'

'Bingo,' she said with a shaky laugh as she realised the truth of what he'd said. 'Scared is exactly the word.'

'Yeah, I figured,' he said. 'I guess that's the reason I've been hard on you. I didn't want to give you too much time to worry about what was happening.' He took a breath. In the dim light, she could see the grim set of his mouth. 'And you were right about my avoiding your questions, Jessie. I should have answered them. You're entitled to know the truth.'

'The truth?' she repeated.

He nodded. 'You asked me how far we were from Eagle Lake. I don't know how far, Jess. The only thing I do know is that we're not in the Tetons.'

'Then where are we?'

Chad shrugged his shoulders. 'I think we came down in the middle of the Wind River Wilderness but I won't be certain until I get a better look at daybreak.'

'And if this is the ... the Wind River Wilderness? What then?'

'That's the part I didn't want to tell you. It means you can forget about walking to a road.'

'Forget it for tonight, you mean,' she said with more confidence then she felt.

'I mean for quite a while. If I'm right about this place, we're at least five or six days from the nearest road.'

Her eyes widened with disbelief. 'What?'

He nodded. 'It won't be easy. This is rough country, Jessie, but we'll be OK if we keep our heads. I've spent a lot of time camped in worse terrain than this.'

She shook her head and stared up at him, trying to see his face in the darkness, fighting against a sudden flutter of panic.

'But ... but they'll find us,' she said quickly. 'You filed a flight plan, didn't you? And you spoke to air controllers on the radio ... Everbody knows where we are.'

'Nobody knows where we are,' Chad said bluntly. 'Our flight plan called for a direct route to Eagle Lake. We got blown pretty far off course, and we lost radio contact before I could tell anybody what was happening.'

'You mean ... you mean we're on our own?'

'The thing to remember is that I've been in country like this before. If you do as I tell you, we'll be fine. I promise.'

She took a deep breath. How could he promise such a thing? But he'd promised he'd land them safely, and he had. And he'd promised to get them ashore, and he had. She laughed shakily. 'Well then, I don't have much choice, do I? What do we do first?'

He breathed a sigh of relief. 'That's the girl. First, we go back to the clearing and build a fire. It's going to get pretty cold tonight. The we'll have dinner.'

'Dinner? Are you kidding?'

He chuckled softly. 'Nope. I've got some dried fruit and candy in my pack. Some instant coffee and bouillon cubes, too. Emergency rations, you might say.' His arm tightened around her. 'Trust me,' he said quietly. 'I'll take care of you.'

Trust him, she thought. She'd heard that phrase before, from people in the business, from men she'd dated. And it always had left the brassy taste of hypocrisy in her mouth. Chad's arm slipped from her waist and his hand closed around hers. She held it tightly as she followed him through the forest. Why, she wondered, did the words sound so different this time?

CHAPTER FIVE

JESSICA peered across the little clearing, watching Chad from half-closed eyes as she had been for the past few minutes. She'd been careful not to shift position or alter her breathing, although she wasn't quite sure why she was so reluctant to let Chad know she was up. He'd been organising the contents of his backpack and boiling water for coffee, moving with an economy of motion and easy grace that was pleasing to the eye. After a bit, she began to feel guilty about watching him so stealthily, and between that and the vague discomfort of awakening with a strange man in your bedroom, even if your bedroom was a clearing in a forest, it had become almost impossible to say a simple 'good morning'.

Get it over with, coward, she told herself, and before allowing herself any more time to think about it, she stretched her arms and faked a yawn.

'Good morning,' Chad said immediately, turning towards her. 'Did you sleep well?'

She nodded her head. 'Fine.'

He smiled. 'Do you always sleep all curled up like that?'

So, she thought, she hadn't been the only one doing the watching. She ignored the reminder of the intimacy of their sleeping arrangements. Not so intimate, really. They'd been on opposite sides of the smouldering fire, each in his or her own bed of leaves and pine branches. There had been plenty of space . . . A sudden, dream-like image flickered into her mind and she frowned.

'I'm glad to see that the sun's shining,' she said

briskly, sitting up and pushing aside the nylon tarpaulin he had given her the night before. 'Everything looks a lot better in the daylight.'

He rose to his feet. 'Some things always look great,' he said.

'Well, that's because you like the wilderness . . .'

'That, too,' he said with a quick smile. She blushed and he dusted off the seat of his jeans. 'I'm going to get washed up, Jessie. I'll be back in a few minutes.'

She nodded her head and watched as he headed through the trees and down the ridge. Then she scrambled to her feet. Had that little remark about some things looking great been meant for her? It didn't seem very likely, she thought, running her fingers through her hair. There were bits of twigs and leaves tangled in her dark curls and she was sure her eyes were puffy— they almost always were this time of year because of her hay fever, although, come to think of it, she hadn't sneezed once since the crash. Maybe it was the altitude. Or maybe it was the fact that she hadn't had a cigarette since . . .

Well, there wasn't much sense in dwelling on that, she thought firmly, shaking out the tarpaulin and then folding it neatly. Her cigarettes were at the bottom of the lake along with everything else. Even her make-up was gone. About the only worthwhile thing she'd hung on to was the little instant focus, instant everything camera she'd brought on the spur of the moment. It wasn't anything like the cameras that had been destroyed in the crash, but it was better than nothing. In the confusion and excitement, she'd forgotten all about it until last night when she'd decided to use her bag for a pillow. Finding the camera inside it, and the five rolls of 36 exposure, high-speed colour film safe in their little plastic containers had been wonderful. She'd patted them happily and then fallen asleep despite the hard, cold ground.

Actually, sleeping on the ground hadn't been quite as uncomfortable as she'd expected. In fact, she thought, smothering a yawn, she'd slept rather well . . . The fuzzy dream memory floated into her mind again, more clearly this time, although it was still uncertain and without substance. Had she actually awakened during the night, shivering with cold? She might have; it wasn't all that unlikely, in spite of the double layer of sweaters she'd worn and the nylon tarpaulin. Jessica had a sudden, vivid image of Chad beside her, drawing her into his arms, holding her close in the warmth of his embrace . . .

Her cheeks flamed with colour. How could a dream—and it was a dream, of course it was—how could a dream seem so real? She crossed the little clearing and laid the folded tarpaulin beside his backpack.

'The bottomless pit,' she'd dubbed the pack when Chad had produced a plastic-wrapped packet of matches and an old metal canteen from its depths. The pack had also provided their dinner of raisins and nuts, along with instant coffee and bouillon cubes to add to the water he'd boiled in the battered canteen cup.

'All the pleasures of home,' he'd said with a grin, handing her the cup filled with coffee.

'Almost,' she'd answered, giving him a grateful smile. 'Is it always this black?' she added, looking up at the sky.

'Blacker. There aren't any stars tonight but at least there's some moonlight. Sorry there's no sugar for that coffee.'

Jessica shook her head and spread her fingers over the hot metal, savouring the warmth and familiar smell of the coffee.

'Don't apologise. I'm still amazed that we've got coffee at all.' She sipped at the dark liquid and then glanced up at the sky again. The moon was chasing through the clouds, its pale underbelly a faint glow against the blackness of the night. The surrounding forest had come alive with a billion sounds.

She drew closer to the fire and shivered. 'I'll never fall asleep,' she said positively, handing the cup to Chad. 'Not even for a minute.'

'Coffee too strong?' he asked innocently.

'I wish that was the reason,' she said. 'What are all those things I keep hearing?'

He chuckled softly and took the cup from her hand. 'Do you really want to know?'

'Good thinking,' she said quickly. 'Don't tell me. I never would have believed it would be this noisy in the middle of nowhere.'

'This isn't noisy, Jessie,' he laughed. 'Noisy is what keeps me wide awake all night in a city hotel room. How can anybody sleep while horns blow and brakes squeal and sirens wail?'

'All that fades into the background after a while. You're just not used to city sounds.'

He handed the cup of coffee back to her and smiled. 'I couldn't have said it better myself. You're just not used to the sound of silence.'

'Silence, huh? Is that what you call it! I never heard so much chattering and snorting and shuffling. I keep expecting something to scream or hoot or howl . . .'

'Something will,' he laughed, 'but you won't hear it. You'll be fast asleep before that part of the symphony starts.'

'That's not exactly what I wanted to hear,' said Jessica quickly. 'You could have been kind and assured me there weren't any sounds like those.'

'You're perfectly safe, Jessie. Believe me, the creatures in the forest don't want anything to do with you, either.'

'Does that go for the bugs, too?' she asked, shifting carefully on the leafy bed he'd made her.

'It's too late in the season for bugs. Well, for most of them, anyway,' he added with a quick smile. 'Besides, you don't have to bother with them until you've been formally introduced.'

'I have absolutely no intention of bothering them. I just hope they don't want to widen their circle of friends.'

Chad stirred the dark red embers of the fire with a blackened stick. 'They won't if you're asleep,' he said reasonably.

'Well,' she said cautiously, 'I'll try. But I'm not sure I'm going to be able to sleep. My body's tired, but my head keeps reminding me that I'm lying on the cold, hard ground in the dark of the night in the middle of a forest on the top of a mountain . . .'

'I'll bet you sleep like a baby. Go on, Jessie. Close your eyes and relax. No monster is going to sneak up on you, I promise.'

There he went again, she had thought, smothering a yawn, making promises . . . It had been the last conscious thought she'd had before tumbling into a dreamless sleep, unless, of course, you counted that middle of the night bit of imagination working overtime when she had thought she'd been in Chad's arms, burrowing sleepily against the hard warmth of him . . .

'I'm back.' She turned at the sound of his voice. He smiled as he stepped into the clearing and dumped an armload of small branches beside the dead fire. 'Sorry if I woke you before. I tried to be quiet.'

She shook her head and ran her fingers through her hair again, trying to smooth and shape it, painfully aware of her unwashed, unmade-up early morning face and the fuzzy taste in her mouth. Chad, she noticed, looked bright-eyed and ready for the day, except for the shadowy beginning of a beard on his face.

'You didn't wake me,' she said quickly. 'I was up . . .' He glanced at her and she hesitated and laughed self-consciously. 'OK, OK, I wasn't. I guess I managed to sleep a bit after all.'

He squatted beside the remains of the fire and began to rearrange the kindling and branches.

'Yeah, I thought you might have dozed off once or twice,' he said casually, digging in his pocket for the matches. 'I figured that's what it meant when you started snoring.'

'I do not snore,' Jessica said indignantly. 'I never——' She sighed as he grinned up at her. 'I didn't, did I? Tell me I didn't.'

Chad brushed his hands off on his jeans. 'OK, you didn't,' he said agreeably. 'You just make strange noises when you sleep.'

She shrugged her shoulders and stuck her hands into her back pockets.

'Well, if I did snore, it's probably because I'm not used to sleeping without a pillow. Not that I'm complaining,' she admitted, watching as he coaxed a tiny flame to life. 'I slept like a log. You were right, I guess. I was a lot more tired than I realised.'

'Yeah, you hardly stirred all night.' He leaned forward and blew on the struggling flame. 'Well, you did wake up briefly at about three in the morning. The cold got to you.'

She stiffened and watched him carefully, but he was concentrating all his energies on the fire.

'Did I?' she said finally. 'I don't remember that at all.' He shrugged his shoulders and added a couple of twigs to the stack. 'I didn't think you would. Once you were warm again, you just drifted right back to sleep.' Suddenly, he lifted his head and his eyes pierced hers. 'You don't remember that, huh?'

Jessica lifted her chin and shook her head. 'No, not at all,' she said quickly, hoping the dancing flames would hide the colour she felt blazing in her cheeks. 'I guess I snuggled right into that tarpaulin you gave me and dozed right off again.'

Chad grinned lazily. 'Sure,' he said easily, 'that must have been it.'

She wanted to look away from him but his eyes held hers, the golden lights in their hazel depths dancing with faint amusement and something more, something she couldn't quite fathom . . . She swallowed drily as he bent his head and broke the electric contact between them.

'Well,' she said in a light voice, 'the sleeping accommodations in this hotel weren't bad, but the plumbing leaves a lot to be desired. I'd give anything for a toothbrush and some soap and a sink.'

'Anything?'

She nodded her head. 'Anything.'

He smiled as he got slowly to his feet. 'We should have a drum roll here,' he said, holding his hands out to her, fingers spread, 'and a spotlight.' Slowly, he rotated his hands before him. 'Abbracadabra,' he said in an overly dramatic, hushed voice. 'The Great O'Bryan promises that, at no time, will his hands ever leave his wrists.'

It was impossible not to smile in return. 'OK, what's this all about?'

'A demonstration of woodland magic, ma'am. Will a volunteer from the audience kindly note the absence of charcoal smudges on my fingers? And the teeth are shiny, ma'am. Care to check more closely and verify that?'

'What I'll verify is that you're crazy,' Jessica laughed. 'You're not going to tell me you have tubes of toothpaste and bars of soap in that bottomless pit you call a backpack, are you?'

'No, sorry about that. Even the old pit has its limits. But fine sand is a great substitute for soap. And I'll personally cut you a terrific aspen twig toothbrush that you can use down by the lake.' He waggled his eyebrows in an exaggerated leer. 'Now, aren't you sorry you said you'd give me anything I wanted for that information?'

'Well, I . . .'

'Nope, it's too late to back out. You're not a welsher, are you, Jess?'

'Well, no,' she said uncomfortably, for some unaccountable reason suddenly remembering the phantom feel of his arms around her in the dark, small hours of the night. 'No, I'm not, but . . .'

'Good. Then you won't object to collecting the next batch of kindling.'

'Kindling? But . . .' She let out her breath and shook her head. 'No problem,' she said lightly. 'Just give me five minutes.'

The fact that he would trust her to do precisely what had got her in trouble the night before filled her with pleasure. It was like being given a vote of confidence and she knew he'd meant it as such. She smiled as she accepted an aspen twig from him and then she set off through the trees.

No question about it, she thought as she started down the ridge. The cowboy was a bit more complicated than she'd expected. He certainly had a disconcerting way of putting her off balance every now and then. He wasn't dull company, that was for sure. And even if he might have been the last man she'd take to the ballet at Lincoln Center, he was the first one—the only one, in fact—

she'd want to be with if she were marooned or
shipwrecked or whatever it was they were. He knew as
much about this forsaken place as she knew about safety
in the subways. She smiled as she pictured him loping
through the city streets. He'd be as out of place there as
she was here. But he'd look pretty good no matter where
you plonked him down, with that square jaw and those
terrific eyes and those broad shoulders and lean hips . . .

'What is wrong with you, Jessie?' she said aloud.

She shook her head and stepped out of the trees at the
bottom of the ridge. The lake sparkled under the sun, its
waters calm and deep, deep blue in the clear morning
light. It looked altogether different with no wind to riffle
its surface. There was, of course, no sign of their plane.
There was nothing to show that they or anyone else had
ever been here, except for the tiny yellow dinghy tied to
a sapling at the shore. The lake, even the mountains
surrounding it, had a primal, lonely beauty.

Jessica knelt on a flat rock and scooped up a handful of
fine-grained sand. She cupped her hands and scooped
up some of the lake water, gasping at its chill kiss. Chad
had been right—the slight abrasiveness of the sand left
her skin feeling clean and smooth. She splashed some
water on her face, then repeated the action with more
vigour, knowing that she was washing away whatever
remained of her make-up and that its replacement lay at
the bottom of the lake.

She sat back on her heels, shivering as a breeze played
across the water and touched her damp skin. She had a
sudden, all too vivid picture of the little plane lying
under all that cold, cold water. For a few moments, she'd
almost forgotten the reality of their situation. Thanks to
Chad's ingenuity, they'd had a relatively pleasant
evening and morning, but even he couldn't keep making
magic for ever. They had to find a way out of this place.

Not that she knew what place this was. She hadn't remembered to ask Chad if he'd managed to figure it out, she thought as she scrubbed at her teeth with the aspen twig. How could she have forgotten something so important? The answer to that one was easy. She hadn't asked the question because she didn't want to risk hearing the answer. He'd already said he thought they were in the—what was it he'd called it?—the Wind River something or other, and that, if they were, it was five or six days to a road. Jessica tossed aside the aspen twig and wiped her hands on her jeans. He couldn't have said that, she told herself firmly. No way. No place was five or six days from a road, not in the twentieth century, not in the good old USA.

She sighed and got to her feet. First things first, her grandmother had always said, and it was good advice. And the first thing she wanted right now was a cup of hot coffee, which meant it was time to stop daydreaming and gather some kindling. There was a sudden glimmer on the lake and a fish jumped free of the water, its iridescent body knifing into the blue sky and then back into the darker lake. A shadow skimmed across the lake and Jessica lifted her eyes upward. There was a bird soaring overhead, its broad, feather-fringed wings barely moving as it caught and rode the wind.

Lord, she thought suddenly, how beautiful this place was. Even the wild peaks rising all around her had a desolate beauty to them.

'Takes your breath away, doesn't it?'

She spun around in surprise. 'How do you manage that? One second you aren't there and the next second you are. I never hear you at all.'

Chad smiled and shrugged his shoulders. 'Years of practice, I guess. When you spend a lot of time outdoors, you learn to move quietly.'

'You could have a terrific career in Central Park after dark,' she laughed. 'Mugging people, I mean,' she added in response to his puzzled expression. 'You see, you know how to walk silently outdoors, and so I mentioned Central Park,' she said with deliberate care. 'That's in New York, in Manhattan, and it's got a reputation for being a bad place at night ...'

'I know precisely where Central Park is,' he said quietly. 'It's unfortunate it isn't safe after dark, because the Ramble and Sheep Meadow must be pretty at night. Of course, when they do Shakespeare in the park or when the Philharmonic plays during the summer it's safe enough, at least it was the last time I went to a concert. They did Beethoven's Seventh that night. That's a famous symphony, by the way, a piece of classical music written in four parts for an orchestra ...'

'For heaven's sake, I know what a symphony is. I'm not stupid ...' A crimson rush flooded her cheeks and she put her hand to her mouth. 'I'm so sorry, Chad,' she murmured as she realised how deliberately and cleanly he'd returned her jibe with one of his own. 'I didn't mean to sound so ... so ...'

'Condescending? Superior? Snobbish?'

'All of those,' she said quickly. 'Really, I just thought you weren't familiar with the city. I forget you said you'd been there on business. I ...'

'No, I'm the one who should apologise, Jessie. After all, I must seem pretty much a—what did you call me?— a cowboy, right? And that's OK, you know. Cowboys are pretty decent guys.'

But he looked anything but apologetic, she thought, standing there with his hands on his hips. There was an edge to his voice that added to her embarrassment.

'Oh, I'm sure of it,' she said. 'It's just that I never

think of someone like that ... I mean, someone like you ...'

He smiled grimly. 'I bet you don't.'

'Look, I simply meant that you don't look like a man who'd be familiar with the ins and outs of New York, that's all. I ...'

'How come you city people are so quick to categorise everybody? Especially when you all seem to run around in costumes.'

Jessica tilted her head and stared up at him. 'What does that mean?' she asked carefully.

Chad shrugged his shoulders. 'You know what I mean, Jessie. You do it, too.'

'Jessica,' she said. 'That's my name, if you don't mind. And no, I don't know what you mean. Why don't you tell me?'

'Look, I don't want to quarrel with you. I ...'

'I'm not quarrelling. I'm just asking you to explain what you meant by that remark.'

'Come on, lady,' he said, his voice rough with impatience. 'I got a good look at you yesterday. There you were, on your way out to the Old West, you thought, and so you wore your Old West outfit. That leather vest, those leather trousers, those asinine boots ...'

'I didn't expect to end up in the middle of nowhere when I started out yesterday. My clothes would have been fine for Eagle Lake Lodge ... Besides, aren't you the one who's being snobbish now? People shouldn't be judged by their clothing, should they?'

Chad shook his head. 'Fashion co-ordinator,' he said. 'Is that really what you do for a living?'

Jessica snorted angrily. 'For heaven's sakes, we've been over all this before. Yes, that's what I do. I'm not ashamed of it, either. I may not be saving the world or anything like that, but my job is an honest one . . .'

'You don't know how I laughed one time when I was in New York and everybody was into their Western glitter phase, I guess you'd call it. All those urban cowboys parading around in jeans so tight they'd split if they ever had to do any real work in them, the women wearing silver and turquoise jewellery that was probably stamped "Made in Taiwan" on the back . . . Doesn't it bother you at all to be part of that, Jessie?'

'My name is not Jessie,' Jessica said quickly, ignoring the little voice deep within her that had almost whispered agreement. 'Dressing up makes people happy. What's wrong with that?'

'What's wrong with it is that there are better things to spend money on than . . . than costumes, especially when all those city folks who want to look like they're roughing it won't be happy until they pave over every inch of grass on this planet.'

'You're a fine one to talk about categorising people,' she said angrily. 'You don't know anything about what I want.'

'Sure I do. You want to play at roughing it without getting your hands dirty.'

'You really have a wonderful opinion of us "city folks", don't you?'

Chad put his hands on his hips. 'Give me one good reason why I should.'

She took a deep breath and her eyes locked with his. 'You know what your problem is, cowboy? We intimidate you, that's what. We have creativity and drive and that makes you nervous. You don't need either one to ride horses. All you need is a strong back and . . . You let go of me,' she hissed, twisting under the sudden bite of his hands. 'Stop that . . .'

His fingers dug into her shoulders as he pulled her

towards him. 'You think you've got it all figured out, haven't you, Miss Howard? Cowboys are just dumb muscle, right? Only guys in three-piece suits who sit behind desks are worth knowing.'

His face was bent to hers. She could see a muscle twitch in his jaw. Suddenly, she was very aware of their isolation.

'No, I didn't say that——'

'You didn't have to say it. Believe it or not, I've got enough brains to figure it out for myself.'

She swallowed hard and tried to smile. 'Look, I never said you didn't have brains. It must be ... it must be interesting work, being a cowboy. And ... and I know there's more to it than just riding horses,' she added lamely, somehow knowing each word only made things worse and yet unable to stop her stumbling speech. 'After all, you're a pilot, too. Well, sure. I mean, some ranches are big, right? Somebody has to know how to drive a car or fly a plane or ... I don't mean that the way it sounds, of course. Everybody knows how to drive a car. I mean, it's not that hard so that only one or two of you could do it ... No, no, that's not what I mean at all. Cowboys are ...'

'They're human,' Chad said quietly. His hands fell from her arms and he shook his head. 'That's all anybody is.'

She wrapped her arms around herself and kneaded the places his fingers had grasped, wondering in some distant part of her mind if she'd be black and blue tomorrow. At least, he'd calmed down.

'Well, sure they are,' she said quickly. 'I know that. I have nothing against cowboys. I'm sure you do an important job ...'

He grimaced in disgust and snorted softly. 'Jesus, Jessica Howard, you are incredible.'

He turned on his heel and walked away from her, heading up the rise with quick, long strides. Jessica watched him for a second and then she scrambled after him.

'Look, I'm sorry. Really. I didn't mean to knock your profession. I ...'

He turned so suddenly that she almost collided with him. 'My profession, Miss Howard,' he said, enunciating each word with care, 'is that of wildlife biologist.'

'What?'

He smiled grimly. 'Ruins the whole thing, doesn't it, Jessie? Here you had me pegged for a dumb cowhand ...'

'No, I didn't. I ...'

'No?' His smile became more wolfish. 'Tell me, Miss Howard, would you have gone to such careful lengths to explain Central Park to me if you'd known I had a PhD in biology?'

'A PhD in biology?' she repeated dumbly.

'And a pilot's licence. That's why your agency hired me. They wanted somebody who could not only ferry things in and out of Eagle Lake but who knew something about the flora and fauna of the Tetons.' He laughed unpleasantly. 'It's amazing how impressed Easterners get when a guy knows the difference between a coyote and a squirrel.'

'You mean—you mean all this time you've been letting me ...' Jessica took a deep breath. 'How could you let me make a fool of myself that way?'

'You didn't need any help from me, Miss Howard. You did just fine, all by yourself from the minute we met.'

'Oh, for God's sake, spare me the lecture, will you?'

'You've been glad to have a cowboy with you since we got here, haven't you? Somebody who could save your pretty neck. I'll bet none of your urban cowboys could do that.'

'No more than you could survive in a three-piece suit, sitting behind a desk,' Jessica said icily.

'At least herding cows has a purpose,' Chad answered. 'But you wouldn't understand that.'

'You said you were a biologist ...'

'Lord, I don't believe you, lady. I am a biologist. I was simply trying to make a point about value judgements, that's all. I'm just tired of having the world run by citified snobs who run it for their benefit.'

She was looking at him as if he'd lost his mind. Well, he thought, maybe he had. Only a lunatic would stand here in the middle of nowhere, arguing against a system he'd been bucking for years, with a woman who wasn't really responsible for it. And what did he care what she thought, anyway? A week from now, she'd just be a memory ...

A strident cry overhead made them both look up. A wedged flight of geese was flying towards the lake, their calls echoing weirdly in the mountain silence.

'It's getting late,' Chad said abruptly. 'We'd better get moving. We've wasted too much time as it is.'

He started up the ridge. There was no choice but to follow him, and, after glaring at his retreating back, that was what Jessica did.

'Have you worked out where we are?' she asked sullenly.

He nodded. 'Where I figured. The Wind River Wilderness.'

Her heart seemed to turn over. 'You mean ... you mean it really will take five or six days to walk to a road? I just can't believe that.'

Chad's rough laughter drifted back to her on a gust of wind. 'Good,' he said, 'because I may have estimated wrong. If those clouds mean business, there's an early snow moving in. If that happens, getting out of here at all might be a miracle.'

Jessica groaned softly. He had his miracles mixed up. The real miracle would be if they could find a way to keep from killing each other.

CHAPTER SIX

THE narrow trail wound up the mountainside, through stands of lodgepole pine and aspen. It was a game trail, Chad had said, used by deer, bear, and elk. Even the names of those creatures had made Jessica feel uncomfortable; for the first hour, she kept glancing over her shoulder, but the only animal she saw was a squirrel scurrying across a pine deadfall.

The possibility of meeting some wild thing on the trail didn't seem half as important after a while as the way her legs ached from ankle to thigh and the way her breath wheezed in her labouring lungs. The sun was a faded yellow disc hanging in a watery blue sky and the air was cool and crisp, but she was sweating hard from the unaccustomed exertion.

By the time they'd left the lake and the birch clearing far below, Jessica was past admiring the spectacular mountain peaks rising all around them. Even the red and gold leaves, clinging to the aspens like flame, lost their appeal. She managed the energy to pull out her little camera at the start of their climb and snapped off several shots. She'd expected Chad to make some biting remark about her wasting time—she'd stepped off the trail once or twice to get the best pictures—but he'd never even noticed.

She paused just long enough to drag a deep breath into her lungs. He hadn't noticed anything, she thought, watching as he moved steadily up the trail ahead of her. He never slowed down, never stumbled over rocks or branches or his own feet the way she did. And he never turned around to see if she was beind him. She was, but just barely, she reminded herself grimly as she started upwards again. Every now and then she lost sight of him around a bend in the trail and then she'd scramble like crazy, puffing like a steam locomotive until she spotted him ahead of her again. But she wasn't about to ask Chad O'Bryan to slow down. She'd be damned if she asked him anything. He seemed to feel the same way, which was fine with her. He hadn't said a word in at least two hours, not since he'd shouldered his pack and headed out of the birch tree clearing.

'Time to get moving,' he'd said without preamble. 'I want to cover as much ground as possible.'

'Where are we going?'

'Out of here,' he'd said in the patient tone people used with puppies and small children. 'I'm going to set a steady pace, Miss Howard. Tell me if you can't manage it.'

She'd squared her shoulders and tilted her chin up. 'Don't worry about me, Mr O'Bryan,' she'd said coolly. 'I'll be fine.'

Well, that hadn't turned out to be completely accurate, she thought, stumbling over a tree root. But she wasn't going to give him the satisfaction of buckling under the demanding pace he'd set. She was every bit as tough as he was and she'd prove it— even if it killed her. Anyway, he had to stop soon. Nobody could keep this up for ever, not even the cowboy who, she was sure, was determined to prove she was nothing but a soft piece of useless, citified fluff.

'Ooof!' Jessica drew in her breath as a sharp pain lanced through her foot. 'Damn,' she said, bending down and rubbing her toes through the canvas sneaker.

'Are you all right?'

No, she thought, I am not all right. I just stubbed my

toes on a chunk of this mountain ...

'Fine,' she said as he came down the trail towards her. 'I just tripped over something.'

Chad watched in silence as she bent over her foot again and then he shrugged free of his pack.

'It's time for a break, anyway. Sit down for a minute and get your breath, Miss Howard.'

Hallelujah, she thought. He's human.

'I'm fine,' she repeated, forcing a polite smile to her face as he settled down on a fallen tree. 'You don't have to stop on my account.'

'I'm not,' he said evenly. 'I need a breather. I'm going to relax, even if you're foolish enough not to.' He dug through his pack and then held the canteen out to her. 'You probably need some water.'

Not if you don't, cowboy, she told herself. 'No, not at all,' she said quickly. 'I'm not the least bit thirsty.'

'Suit yourself.' She drew in her breath as he tilted the canteen to his mouth, swallowing thirstily as she watched him drink, but she said nothing. 'We have some rough climbing ahead of us,' he said finally. 'It might be a good idea to prepare for it.'

Rough climbing? she thought incredulously, wondering what it was he thought they'd just done. But she simply nodded her head and shrugged her shoulders.

'Don't worry about me.'

'I'm not,' he said sharply. 'I'm worried about me. I want to get some more distance under my belt before we have to stop and make camp.'

'How much further do we have to go?'

Chad wiped the top of the canteen and shrugged. 'A couple of miles. Not very far.'

'A couple of miles?' she repeated carefully. 'Well, that's ... that's not bad. Maybe I will sit down for just a minute, though. I—er—I want to fix my laces anyway.'

'I know I'm pushing you, Miss Howard ...'

'No, you're not,' she said quickly, sitting down on the fallen tree as far from him as the limited space permitted. 'I'm used to exercise.'

'Are you, indeed?'

She nodded. 'I've kept pace with you, haven't I?'

Chad offered her the canteen again. After a barely perceptible pause, she snatched it from him.

'You wouldn't have, if I hadn't set a pace you could manage.'

She spluttered over the mouthful of cold lake water. 'What? Are you trying to tell me you slowed down for me?' She wiped her chin and laughed unpleasantly. 'Come on, now ...'

'I heard you huffing and puffing and groaning to yourself, and I knew I'd better slow down if I wanted to get anywhere.' He took the canteen from her and tucked it back into his pack. 'Jogging in—what's that place called? You know, that park in Manhattan. Jogging there isn't the same as climbing this mountain, is it?'

She gritted her teeth, determined not to pick up the verbal gauntlet he'd thrown between them.

'I do more than jog. I belong to a health club. I work out on a Nautilus machine and I do some very tough aerobics.' Well, she thought, it wasn't exactly a lie. The fact that she hadn't done any of those things more than a couple of times over the past year or two was none of his business.

Chad grinned mirthlessly. 'Nautilus machine, hmm? And aerobics—is that where everybody wears those little bits of stretchy stuff and bounces up and down to music?'

'It's not at all easy,' Jessica said stiffly. 'If you ever tried it, you'd know that.'

'Yeah, I can see you people now, all decked out in

some uniform designed by a guy who probably never worked up a real sweat in his life.'

'Don't tell me,' she said wearily. 'You lift weights and you run five miles a day and you do it all wearing baggy grey sweats that you've had for at least ten years. But your running shoes are the best on the market. Right?'

Chad's eyes narrowed. 'What are you getting at?'

She closed her eyes and rotated her head tiredly. 'Nothing, nothing at all.'

'Come on, Miss Howard. There was a message there somewhere. I'm not dense . . .'

Her eyes snapped open. 'Did it ever occur to you that your outfit's as much a uniform as the one you picture me in?'

'Don't be ridiculous. My sweats and my Reeboks are for real work-outs. Why, I can tell what a man's like just by looking at his . . .'

A triumphant smile spread over Jessica's face. 'Really?' she purred. 'How interesting.'

Chad flushed darkly and got to his feet. 'The point is, Miss Howard, you don't need to wear fancy outfits and join fancier gyms to develop a healthy body. Some of us were into physical fitness long before it became fashionable.' He hoisted the pack to his shoulders and stepped across the fallen tree. 'Come on,' he said gruffly, 'let's move out. The weather's still got me worried.'

He started up the trail without a backward glance. Jessica smothered a groan as she stood up. Point scored, Jessie, she told herself. Too bad she was too tired to savour it. Actually, he wasn't that far off the mark. She shifted her bag strap, trying to keep it from digging into her shoulder. Not that she'd ever admit it to him, of course, but one of the reasons she hadn't gone back to the health club after her first few visits was because she felt out of place sweating and straining amid all those flawless people who never strained, much less sweated and who always seemed to be together at rallies for this year's cause or charity, as if they had no existence outside their group.

She was sure the cowboy had been working out for years. The cowboy—correction, she reminded herself, stepping across a downed tree—he was Dr O'Bryan, although it was hard to think of him that way. But it wasn't hard to think of him as a man who kept himself fit. He was all lean muscle and flat planes. And it was easier to picture him in an old sweatsuit than in chartreuse satin shorts and a matching sweatband, prancing up and down to a heavy metal beat in Swenson's mirrored gym. She choked back a sudden peal of laughter.

Chad heard the muffled sound drift up the trail. It sounded as if she was coughing or maybe smothering a laugh. Not that it mattered; this wasn't a popularity contest. Jessica Howard didn't have to like him. All she had to do was keep up the pace—which, surprisingly enough, she'd managed to do so far. In fact, she'd been doing all right from the beginning. Not that he'd tell that to her, of course. The woman was all ego. She needed compliments about as much as a bull needed milking . . .

'Ahhh . . .'

Jessica's cry of pain was sudden and shrill, knifing sharply into the stillness of the trail. Chad whirled around at the sound, his heart racing. Jesus, she was down! He tossed his pack aside and ran back towards her.

'Jessie? Jessie!' He fell to his knees beside her. 'Are you all right?'

She nodded her head as his arm went around her

shoulders. 'Yes, I'm OK,' she murmured. 'I just tripped or something.'

Chad lifted her gently and she sat up, leaning into the curve of his arm.

'Are you sure there's nothing broken?' She nodded her head and he let out his breath. 'When I heard you yell, I thought ...' His arm tightened around her. 'I thought ...' Her eyes met his. The seconds stretched between them and then Chad's arm fell away from her shoulders. 'I thought you might have broken something.'

Jessica let out her breath. 'Yes, of course. You were afraid I'd slow us down.'

'We can't afford any delays, Miss Howard. I told you, there's snow coming. We've got to get to shelter before then.'

Inexplicably, angry tears filled Jessica's eyes. She blinked them back and turned her head away from him.

'I won't hold you up. I ... ouch!'

'What's the matter?' he asked sharply.

'I ... nothing. I'm fine.'

Chad pushed her back to the ground. 'Let me see that foot,' he said.

'I'm OK.'

'Let me be the judge of that.'

'Really, I know what I'm doing ...'

'If you'd known what you were doing, you wouldn't have fallen in the first place. Does that hurt?' She shook her head as he prodded gently at her ankle. 'How about that?' She shook her head again. Weren't you watching your footing?'

'I ... I don't know,' she said. 'I thought I was being careful ... I already said I was sorry.'

'Never mind that now. Tell me if I'm hurting you.'

She watched as he untied the sneaker and peeled off

her sock. Lord, but he was angry, she thought, watching his face. He was glaring at her foot as if it were his mortal enemy. Well, she thought, she couldn't much blame him. What he probably wanted to do was glare at her. There was no point in kidding herself; no matter how she tried, she was slowing him down. And even she could feel the approaching snow now; the sky was thick with white clouds and there was a sharp, cold smell in the air.

Chad was moving her ankle from side to side. What a strange man he was, she thought, watching his face from under half-lowered lashes. He was tough as these mountains, yet so gentle that she could barely feel the touch of his hand on her ankle. She thought of the way he'd looked at the lake that morning, watching the geese flying high above them, and her throat contracted painfully. He wasn't tough at all; he was strong, strong enough to have saved their lives a dozen times over since yesterday. You couldn't hurt a tough man but you could hurt a strong one, which was what she'd managed to do this morning when she'd made that clumsy remark about Central Park, not that she'd meant it the way he'd taken it—although the truth was she'd been taking subtle snipes at him from the start ...

'Ouch,' she said through her teeth as he moved her foot up and down.

Chad looked up sharply. 'Did that hurt?'

'No, not really,' she lied. 'There was just a little twinge. It's OK.'

'Are you sure?' he demanded.

She nodded.

'I hope so. Because if you're not ...'

Tears welled in her eyes again and began to trickle down her cheeks.

'It does hurt, doesn't it?' he asked angrily. 'Damn it, tell me the truth, Jessie.'

'I said it doesn't.'

'Then why are you crying?'

'I . . . I don't know,'she whispered truthfully.

'Your ankle . . .?'

She shook her head. 'It isn't that. I—I guess I just feel useless. I know I'm holding you back.'

He leaned back on his heels. 'Actually, you're doing pretty damned well.'

'You don't have to say something just to make me feel better.'

'Do you really think I would?' A slow smile spread across his face. 'I'm glad to hear your opinion of me's improved.'

She sniffed back her tears and wiped her nose on the back of her hand. 'Am I really doing OK?'

'Are you serious?' She sniffed again and he put his finger under her chin and tilted her face up. 'I thought you'd be up half the night, waiting for something awful to come out of the woods. But you curled right up and went to sleep.'

A faint smile flickered on her mouth. 'I'm not sure if that was courage or exhaustion.'

Chad grinned. 'Yeah,' he said. 'I noticed that you were a pretty sound sleeper except when the cold got to you. But you settled right down again once you were warm enough.'

A pink blush spread across her face as she remembered the phantom feel of a warm, strong embrace.

'Well,' she said defensively, 'I'm not used to sleeping outdoors.'

He grinned again. 'Hell, that wasn't a criticism, Jessie. What I'm trying to say is that you're doing all right.'

She brushed the hair from her eyes and smiled at him. 'For a city slicker, you mean.'

'For anybody who's not used to the wilderness. I can

think of lots of people who'd have trouble getting up this mountain.'

'I told you, I work out. I . . .' She broke off in mid-sentence and sighed. 'Who am I kidding? The only regular exercise I get is when I run for the bus or the subway. I live in dread of the elevator breaking down in my apartment building.' She flashed him a quick, embarrassed smile. 'Isn't that awful? I live on the twelfth floor . . .'

'Twelve floors? I don't blame you.'

'Now you're making fun of me,' she said.

Chad shook his head. 'No, I'm not. You're talking to a man who ate a candy bar for dinner the other night because the restaurant in my hotel was closed and I didn't want to walk a few blocks for a decent meal.'

'You're making that up,' she said slowly. He shook his head and she smiled. 'I can't believe it.'

'Believe it. Given a choice, I can be as lazy as the next guy, Jess. Lazier, maybe. At least, that's what my college room-mate used to tell me when he tried to convince me to clean up my half of the room.'

She smiled and closed her eyes. 'Thank goodness,' she sighed. 'You'll never know how good it is to find out that you're human.'

'I told you that this morning,' he said quietly. 'Remember?'

'Chad, about this morning—I didn't mean to insult you,' she said quickly. 'That thing about Central Park, well, I just wasn't thinking, I . . .'

He shook his head. 'No, it was my fault, Jess. I over-reacted. It's just that, well, I had a rough time in New York last week . . . I had to see some administrative people about a grant I'd applied for, and a couple of them made it pretty clear they'd have felt a lot happier handing out money to one of their own. And then I had dinner with your boss at some place on the east side where they make you hang a tie around your neck before they let you through the door. And your boss made sure he used only one syllable words when he talked to me.'

'Don't tell me,' Jessica sighed. 'He's a nice man, but he thinks anybody born more than five miles from the Brooklyn Bridge is suspect.'

Chad chuckled as he dug his canteen out of his pack. 'Yeah, that's the guy. I think he was surprised to find out that I could string more than three sentences together. Anyway, I'm sorry I jumped all over you.'

She took the cup of water he'd poured and sipped at it gratefully. 'I'll accept your apology if you accept mine,' she said. 'We just got off to a bad start. That thing on the plane ... Well, I've had some unpleasant experiences with men, I mean, I ...'

'You're one hell of a good-looking lady, Jessie. You don't have to explain what happens. I can figure it out without any help.'

The compliment pleased her more than she wanted him to see, and she busied herself re-tying her sneakers.

'Yes, but you were right about how scared I was. And you really did help me.'

'Did I, Jess?'

'Yes,' she said quickly, 'you did. You made me ...' Her words tumbled to a halt as she remembered the unexpected intensity of their kiss. Her eyes lifted to his; he was remembering it too, she could see it in his face. 'Yes,' she said again, knowing she owed him this honest admission. 'You've helped me get through some rough times, Chad.'

He got to his feet and swept off his hat. 'The pleasure's been all mine, ma'am,' he said solemnly. 'We aim to please.' He held his hand out to her. 'How's that ankle feel?'

Jessica clasped his hand and moved forward carefully. There was an immediate twinge in her ankle, but she smiled brightly. 'It's fine,' she said. 'No problem.'

'Are you sure?'

She nodded. 'Absolutely,' she lied.

'Good. There's just a little further to go, Jess. Up that trail another mile or so and then there's a narrow pass to cross.'

'Then what? You said something about shelter.'

He nodded his head and hoisted the pack on to his shoulders. 'I saw some aerial photos of this area a couple of years ago when I was doing a survey on golden eagles. I remember something about a valley beyond the other side of this mountain. At least, I hope I do.'

She picked up her bag and slung it across her shoulder. 'What do you remember?' she asked eagerly. 'Will it help us?'

He nodded. 'If I've got my landmarks straight, we'll find an old cabin where we can get out of the weather for the night. Even at this time of year, the snows can be pretty bad here. But we've got to make tracks if we want to get there and have time to set up camp before the sun goes down. Are you warm enough?'

Jessica glanced down at what she was wearing, a crazy mixture of his jeans, her pink silk blouse, and a heavy fisherman's knit turtleneck of Chad's that hung almost to her knees and nodded.

'I'm fine,' she assured him. 'Not very stylish,' she added with deadpan seriousness, 'but that's OK. Just as long as we don't run into anybody from the *Sunday Times* ...' She looked up and her eyes met his. He grinned and she smiled in return.

'Actually, I think you look kind of cute. And you might just start a new—what's it called? A new fashion statement.'

'Terrific,' she laughed. 'When we get out of this mess, I'll recommend you to the agency. You'd be a great fashion co-ordinator, cowboy.' The name slipped out before she could stop it and she caught her lower lip between her teeth. 'Listen,' she said quickly, 'I didn't mean that in any derogatory way ...'

Chad's eyes narrowed and his mouth set in a grim line. 'Don't call me that again,' he said quietly.

She swallowed drily. 'Chad, I'm sorry. Really. I didn't mean it as an insult ...'

'Come on, Jess. How else could you have meant it?'

She grasped at his sleeve. 'I meant it as a compliment, Chad. Really. I think cowboys are terrific. You know, they're strong and silent and honest and ...'

Chad grinned at her. 'Yeah,' he said. 'So do I. It's the fashion co-ordinator crack I objected to.'

She glanced up at him and then she began to smile. 'You rat,' she said softly. 'You set me up.'

'Don't be silly,' he said with wide-eyed innocence. 'A cowboy's much too honest to set anybody up.'

She caught the quick grin on his face before he moved out on the trail and she smiled as she began the climb up the mountain again. Chad was going more slowly this time; he was always within sight, and it was somehow reassuring to see his long, lean legs in their faded denim jeans and his broad shoulders inside the worn denim jacket just ahead of her. She ached to take out her camera and capture him on film, but that would have meant slowing down. Besides, it took all the effort she could muster to keep moving in spite of the pain in her foot. After a while, he stopped and waited until she caught up to him.

'How's the ankle?'

'It's fine,' Jessica said blithely.

'We can take it a bit easier from this point on. As it is, we're making pretty good time. Maybe I'll have the chance to put together a real dinner tonight.'

'That's right, tease me with visions of steak and hamburger. Raisins are raisins, no matter what you call them.'

He grinned at her. 'I really hate to tell you this, Jess, but we're damned near out of raisins.'

'But you said ...'

'I said I'd make us a real meal. How does stew sound to you?'

'Beef stew?' Her mouth watered at the sound of the word. 'It's not nice to tease the city folk.'

'Rabbit stew. You can pull up some wild onions and I'll fetch up the rabbit.'

'Rabbit?' she repeated carefully. 'I don't ... I couldn't ... Chad, you wouldn't ...'

He shrugged his shoulders. 'I would, but not if you feel that way about it. We'll see if there's a stream or a lake around.' He glanced at her and smiled. 'I assume you're not squeamish about eating trout, Mis Howard.'

She shook her head. 'No, of course not. Fish aren't the same as rabbit.'

'Neither are hamburgers and steaks, I guess. Right?'

'Exactly. I ...' A sudden image of a soft-eyed cow drifted into her thoughts. For the first time in her life, she allowed herself to make the unpleasant connection between a steak and its source. 'I'm afraid I never thought of it that way,' she admitted. 'You're right, of course.'

Chad laughed softly. 'You're learning, Jess. Don't worry. We'll stick with trout and wild onions for the time being.'

She sighed and plodded on up the trail. She certainly was learning, she thought, wincing as she put her weight on her bad foot. And she had the feeling the lessons weren't finished yet.

CHAPTER SEVEN

THE sun was touching the saw-toothed mountain peaks, and shadows were beginning to lengthen across the narrow trail when Chad finally halted and motioned Jessica to his side.

'Are we there?' she gasped as she plodded the last few feet towards him.

He took her hand and helped her up to the rocky ledge on which he was standing. 'Yeah, we sure are. Trail's end, Jessie. Welcome to Coleman's Creek.'

'Coleman's . . .?' She started to echo the name, but the words caught in her throat as she stared into the valley below. Two lines of log cabins stood among tall grass and lodgepole pines. There was an eerie sense of abandonment about the place. The doors to some of the cabins hung open and Jessica had the unpleasant feeling that all the little buildings were staring blindly at the silent valley through the glassless eyes of their broken windows. 'My God,' she whispered, 'it's a town.'

'Well, what's left of one, anyway. This was a pretty prosperous little mining place until the silver petered out along about 1900.'

Jessica nodded her head. Without conscious thought, she moved closer to Chad, who smiled and slid a comforting arm around her waist.

'I guess I should have prepared you for Coleman's Creek, but I wasn't positive I could find it. I didn't want to get your hopes up.'

'But a ghost town . . . in the middle of the wilderness?'

'There are quite a few of them in the Tetons and the

Rockies—towns that sprang up overnight when there was a gold or silver strike and then died when the veins gave out.' His arm tightened around her. 'Want to take a look?'

'I don't know,' she said with a nervous laugh. 'I mean, it doesn't look terribly hospitable, does it?'

'Look, if you'd like to wait for me up here while I check things out . . .'

Jessica shook her head. 'No, thanks,' she said emphatically. 'I'd much rather stick close to you, if you don't mind.'

Chad's hand sought hers and their fingers intertwined. 'My pleasure, ma'am,' he said with a quick smile. 'Let's go take a walk through Coleman's Creek.'

Half-way down the steep hillside, she paused and tilted her head to the side.

'Something's moaning,' she whispered. 'Do you hear it?'

'It's just the wind sighing through the buildings, Jess.'

The eerie sound was repeated and Jessica moved closer to Chad's side. 'Are you sure?'

'Jessie, believe me, there's nothing here that can hurt you.'

'It just seems awfully spooky.'

'Spooky, Miss Howard? Spooky? Is that how you'd describe these busy streets? Watch out for that mule team, ma'am.' She smiled uncertainly as Chad pulled her to the side of the grass-choked path. 'Look lively, there, Miss Howard. This time of day, everybody's coming into town, ready for a ten-cent bath and a twenty-five-cent hot meal.'

'I'd settle for either one,' she said wistfully.

'And you'd have had them,' Chad said gallantly. 'But the Presidential Suite at the Grand Hotel was all booked.' He gestured towards a large, roofless building across the weed-choked dirt street. 'I didn't bother making other arrangements, ma'am. I knew you wouldn't want a common hotel room.'

It was impossible not to smile at him. 'I'm glad you realised that, Mr O'Bryan.'

'As for the hot meal, I phoned ahead to the Never To Be Confused With Mom's Cooking Café over there, indigestion a speciality of the house. Unfortunately, I wasn't able to reserve a table.'

Jessica chuckled softly. 'A pity. I believe they got three stars in the Michelin Guide, didn't they?'

'Four. The Michelin food critic found a piece of real carrot in the ragout and upped the listing on the spot.'

'How could I have forgotten something like that?' she laughed. Suddenly, Coleman's Creek seemed more like a stage set than a ghost town. 'However did you find this place?'

'I told you, I remembered it from an aerial survey. It's not New York City, but it's better than nothing.'

'You're darned right it's not New York. It's ... it's ...' She narrowed her eyes and looked slowly around her. 'You know, I'll bet nobody's ever taken any pictures of all this. And in this light, with those low clouds and the washed-out sun ...' A bright smile flashed across her face as she pulled her little camera from her pocketbook. 'I just wish I had my SLR and a wide-angled lens. But I bet I still get some great shots.'

Chad watched as she brought the camera to her eye and peered into it. 'I've been meaning to ask you about that little toy.'

'Oh, it's not a toy,' she said, snapping off a shot of the overgrown main thoroughfare. 'This little gem is the newest thing in cameras.' She shook her head in admiration and took another quick photograph of the abandoned town. 'I'm just glad I dumped it into my shoulder-bag. If I'd had time to pack it away . . .' She shrugged her shoulders expressively.

'Are you a camera buff, Jessie?'

Jessica gave him a bemused glance and then peered into the camera again. 'What I am is a nut when it comes to photography equipment,' she said. 'I can never resist the newest stuff.' She glanced at Chad and smiled. 'Photography can be an expensive business.'

He eased the pack from his shoulders and flexed his muscles tiredly. 'Now you've got me confused. I thought you said you were a fashion co-ordinator.'

'Well, I am. But that's only until I get my break. That's why I came to New York in the first place . . . Why are you looking at me that way?' she demanded.

'What way?'

'Come on, Chad, I know there's something . . .'

He pushed his hat back on his head and grinned. 'You won't like it.'

'Try me.'

'Well, I was just thinking it's nice to know you want to do something real with your life.' He grinned as her chin lifted defensively. 'I told you you wouldn't like it.'

'What I do now is real. Just because you don't understand the fashion industry . . .' She stared at him through narrowed eyes. 'Are you laughing at me?'

'Lordy, Miss Howard, ma'am, you sure are pretty when you get mad.'

His teasing drawl took the fight out of her and she laughed softly. 'Only when I'm mad?' she said. 'I'm disappointed.'

The words slipped out before she had time to think about them. For goodness' sakes, she thought in amazement, I'm flirting with the man! Here they were in the middle of absolutely nowhere and she was behaving as if they'd just been introduced at a party. Except she never behaved that way at a party—but then, she'd never run into anybody remotely like Chad O'Bryan, either. And she wouldn't, not back in New York, not at the cocktail parties given by Allen Associates. Somehow, she couldn't picture Chad with a plastic glass filled with warm wine in one hand and a soggy, cheese-topped cracker in the other.

'Your turn,' he said softly.

'My turn? To do what?'

A slow smile spread across his face. 'To tell me why you're looking at me that way.'

She felt the heat rush to her cheeks and she turned away from him. 'Are we really going to stand here talking in the middle of a blizzard?' she asked quickly.

'Not going to tell me, huh?' He laughed softly. 'OK, I'll let you change the subject. Anyway,' he added, glancing up at the few flakes falling lazily from the sky, 'you're right. We should find shelter before this stuff gets heavier.' He bent and hoisted the pack on to his shoulder. 'We might as well take our pick before the rush starts.'

She limped after him towards one of the few cabins that appeared to be intact, pausing beside him at the half-open door. The hinges squealed mournfully as Chad pushed it completely open. A weak patch of sunlight illuminated the dirt floor. Darkness loomed beyond that.

'My God,' Jessica murmured, 'it's black as pitch in there.'

'Let's see if the roof's in one piece.' Chad stepped into the shadowed interior and vanished from view. 'It's not bad, Jess. Come take a look.'

She stepped inside the cabin and moved tentatively across the hard-packed floor, repressing a shudder as she grazed the soft, springy edge of a spider web. As she reached Chad's side, something small and dark scurried past her.

'What was that?'

His arm slid around her. 'Just a mouse, Jessie. You're not afraid of something that tiny, are you?'

She swallowed hard and shook her head. 'No, I'm not afraid of mice. Rats, yes, and snakes and bats and . . .'

'No snakes, I promise. They're cold-blooded creatures and they sleep the winter away. No bats, either. I already looked.'

'I guess I'm not supposed to notice that you left rats off that list, huh?'

Chad smiled and squeezed her shoulder reassuringly. 'Give me a couple of minutes to check the debris inside the fireplace and then I'll let you know, OK? You just stand right there.'

'Believe me, I won't move an inch,' she said.

He touched her hair lightly and then stepped away. She felt vulnerable outside the comforting circle of his arm. She watched as he pulled open the shutters at one of the windows. Light spilled into the cabin. He knelt before the hearth for a moment, then walked around the small room, opening cupboards and peering into the corners. He moved with a kind of animal grace, clearly as much at home in this roughly made place as he had been on the mountain trail. She thought of what it would be like to be in Coleman's Creek with one of the men she sometimes dated in the city—not that one of them would have got this far. The idea was so incongruous that it made her smile. She could just picture Tom in his Italian silk suits or Craig in something in suede and leather that suited the setting . . .

'This is perfect, Jessie,' Chad said, tossing his hat on the dusty table. 'There's not even a sign of anything that

could bother us. In fact, there might even be good news
...' He knelt before the fireplace and peered into it.
'Seems as though somebody's had a fire in here within
the last couple of years,' he grunted, pulling a chunk of
fire-blackened paper out from among the ashes in the
hearth.

Jessica's eyebrows rose. 'Somehow, the possibility of
somebody wandering around here doesn't sound so good
to me,' she murmured, glancing over her shoulder.

'I didn't mean there was anybody here now, Jess. This
place hasn't been touched for a long time. What I was
thinking was that if somebody had holed up here, he
might have left some things behind.' Chad got to his feet
and wiped his hands on his jeans. 'Canned goods,
maybe, or flour. Suppose you see what you can do about
straightening up a little while I check out the other
buildings?'

'You mean ...' She glanced around the cabin and
then she nodded. 'Sure. That's a good idea.'

Chad smiled. 'There's nothing to be afraid of, Jessie,
but you can come with me if you'd rather not stay here
alone.'

She shook her head. 'Don't be silly,' she said briskly.
'You're talking to a New Yorker, remember? Nothing
fazes us.' She smiled and pushed him gently towards the
door. 'Go on, Chad. By the time you get back, I'll have
the floor waxed and the windows washed and the walls
painted and the furniture gleaming.'

He grinned and touched his finger to her nose. 'Don't
forget to put the steak on.'

She smiled at him in return. 'How about if I open a
bottle of Beaujolais?'

Chad laughed and ran his finger down her nose to her
mouth. It was a lightly affectionate gesture but it sent a
tremor spiralling through her.

'I only wish,' he said. 'Maybe I can at least find us some coffee or tea.'

'I'm counting on it,' she said lightly. She watched as he headed out the door and then she shook herself. 'Get to work, Jessie,' she muttered aloud. 'Do something useful.'

There was a tumbled pile of old rags on one of the shelves. Carefully, using two fingers, she pulled out a piece of cloth and turned towards the table, attacking its dusty covering gingerly at first and then with a vengeance. She stood back and admired her handiwork. At least you could see the wood, she thought, which was more than you'd been able to do before.

She grimaced and swung the rag at a spider web hanging from the ceiling. The fragile structure collapsed and she whisked it away. With increasing vigour, she moved about the cabin, dusting the lopsided chair in the corner, the stool beside the table, the cupboard against the far wall. She swung the cloth towards the narrow, wood-slat bed beside the cupboard and her hand stopped in mid-air. A tingling sensation danced down her spine. The thought of spending the long, dark hours of the night in this little room with Chad made the breath catch in her throat, which was silly considering the way they'd been living. Except for a handful of minutes, they hadn't been out of each other's sight.

There was an intimacy about their living arrangements that went beyond anything she'd experienced before. They had eaten together and slept together—a figure of speech, she reminded herself quickly. Until now, she hadn't spent this many consecutive hours with any man, not even the one or two who had been important to her in the past. Relationships that took you from dinner to breakfast and back to dinner again had more disadvantages than benefits.

'What is the matter with you, Jessie?' she whispered. 'Stop being foolish.'

The door swung open and a gust of cold air swept into the room.

'Cabin fever already?' Chad asked with a grin. 'Gotta watch that, Jess. It's a bad sign.'

She laughed self-consciously. 'Hasn't anybody ever told you it's damned disconcerting to have somebody sneak up on you that way? Good grief, Chad, what is all that stuff?'

She hurred towards him as he dropped an armload of cans on the table. 'That, Miss Howard,' he said, 'is dinner. A veritable feast, in fact.'

'Beans?' she asked warily, picking up one of the cans and peering at the darkened label. 'Beans are a feast?'

Chad shrugged his shoulders. 'They are when you consider that it's beans or nothing.'

'How quickly we forget, Dr O'Bryan. You promised me trout for dinner.'

'It's too late. The market's closed.' Chad laughed at her expression. 'I won't have time to try my luck down at the creek, Jessie. I'm afraid it's beans and bannock tonight.'

'Bannock?'

'Yeah. I found some flour, you see, so ...'

'So we'll have bannock. Of course.' She shook her head and smiled. 'I don't suppose you'd mind telling me what bannock is, would you? I mean, I don't know if you wear it or drink it or chew it ...'

'You chew it, and then you compliment the chef.' He smiled and tossed his hat on the table. 'Bannock is trail bread, and I make the meanest batch of it this side of the Rockies.'

Jessica eyed the tins warily. 'But this stuff may have been here for ever, Chad. Is it safe to eat?'

'Just take a look, Jess. No bulges, no holes, nothing but a little rust and dust.' He picked up one of the cans and polished it on his sleeve. 'It hasn't been here more than a couple of years. Coleman's Creek probably had a resident hermit a while back.' He glanced at her and smiled. 'It's not uncommon. There was an old guy who lived in a ghost town in Colorado for almost a decade.'

'But ... if there was a hermit in Coleman's Creek, what happened to him?'

'I don't know. He might have got lost in these mountains or fallen through the ice ... Hey,' he added quickly, seeing the sudden look of fear on her face, 'I bet it was nothing half so dramatic. He probably just moved on.'

'At least he left his beans behind,' Jessica sighed. 'OK, beans and bannock it is. Sounds delicious. To tell the truth, I am absolutely starved.'

'In that case,' Chad said, reaching into his pack, 'You'll be happy to hear we even have dessert.' He grinned and held up a large can with a faded, illegible label. 'Ta ra! Cherries Jubilee, ma'am. How's that sound?'

'Like you've lost your mind,' she said, peering at the can. 'You can't read the label on that thing.'

'OK,' he said agreeably, 'then it's Peach Melba.'

'Sure it is,' she laughed. 'Then again, maybe it's Baked Alaska.'

'Well,' he said, prying open the top of the bean can with the blade of his pocket-knife, 'whatever it is, it's dessert.'

'You'd better hope it's not dog food,' Jessica said wryly.

'Stop looking at the dark side of things, woman. We have a roof over our heads, food for our bellies, and a

stack of dry firewood in the corner. What more do we
need?'

'Some heat,' she said immediately. 'I don't know
about you, but I'm cold.'

Chad nodded. 'Yeah, the sun's going down and the
snow's getting heavier. Let me clear that hearth out a
bit.'

He shrugged out of his denim jacket and squatted on
his heels before the fireplace. She watched in silence as
he reached into its depths, scooping out chunks of wood
and debris and tossing them to the side. He was wearing
an old red and black flannel shirt, its colours faded to soft
pastels. She could see the muscles in his back moving
under the clinging fabric and almost picture how they
would look flexing under his skin. More than once, she'd
run her hand over shoulders and backs that were well
muscled, setting male models into positions as Hans
snapped away with his camera, but she'd never had the
desire to run her hand over a man's back for the sheer,
sensual pleasure of it. But that was what she wanted to do
right now. She wanted to reach down and touch Chad
and have him turn around and touch her ...

'Cabin fever,' she muttered aloud. Chad turned and
looked at her and she cleared her throat. 'I said, I'll get
cabin fever unless I do something useful. Let me help
with those ashes.'

She leaned past him and scooped an empty, charred
can from the back of the fireplace. They worked quietly
for a few minutes, clearing the stone hearth until finally
he leaned back and nodded.

'Good,' he said, wiping his hands on his jeans. 'That
ought to do it.'

'What's next? I hope it's dinner.' She stood up and
made a face as she looked at her hands. 'I don't suppose
there's running water in this place.'

Chad shook his head. 'Sorry.'

'Don't you have any magic formula this time. Dr O'Bryan? You know, like lake water and sand?'

He shook his head again as he rose to his feet. 'No, I'm afraid not. You'll just have to wipe your hands on your jeans.'

'Your jeans, remember?' she said, grinning at him as she rubbed her hands on the seat of her trousers.

He smiled crookedly. 'I've been meaning to tell you, Jessie—you look a lot better in them than I ever did. Of course, I know they're not the latest thing in the fashion world . . .'

Suddenly, she could feel the pulse beating in her throat. 'I'm not the latest thing in the fashion world,' she said quickly. Her hand went to her hair. 'I'm probably a mess . . .'

His fingers closed lightly around her wrist and he shook his head. 'You look beautiful, Jessie,' he said softly.

'I . . . I thought you were going to build a fire,' she remarked inanely.

'In a minute,' said Chad, drawing her towards him.

'But it's cold in here.'

'Second lesson of survival, Jessie,' he said softly. 'Make do with whatever's at hand.'

'Chad,' she said as he pulled her arms around him, 'Chad, what . . .?'

'I'm just being helpful,' he said softly as his arms closed around her. 'There, now. Aren't you warmer?'

His hands were warm and firm on her back. She lifted her hands and put them against his chest; his heart beat was slow and sure beneath her fingers.

'Jessie?' he whispered.

She tilted her head back and looked up at him. His jaw and upper lip looked as if they'd been charcoal-smudged, but she knew it was because he hadn't shaved in two days. Suddenly, she wondered what it would be like to feel the roughness of his beard against the smoothness of her throat. A sudden heat coursed through her body.

'Chad?' she whispered.

'Yes?' The single word was soft and husky.

'Are you making a move on me?'

He smiled lazily. 'I don't know. Am I?'

She had asked the question deliberately, hoping the very bluntness of it would defuse the situation, but his answer only made things more confused. She caught her lower lip between her teeth and cleared her throat.

'This isn't fair,' she said at last.

Chad nodded. 'You're absolutely, positively right, Miss Howard. It isn't.'

'It isn't?' she repeated in a small voice.

He drew her closer. 'I'm at a disadvantage, you know. I mean, if we'd met in Los Angeles or Houston or even New York, at one of those places on Third Avenue where you have to push your way through a hanging jungle of spider plants to get to the bar, I'd know how to deal with you. I'd come on to you so fast your pretty head would spin.'

An unexpected shiver of pleasure ran through her like a shock of electricity.

'How about Canton?' she whispered.

Chad grinned. 'Is that where you're from, Jessie?' She nodded again. 'I'd definitely make a move on you in Canton.'

She smiled up at him. 'Like you did on the plane?'

'No, that was . . .' The protest died and he nodded. 'OK, it's true. I didn't kiss you for therapeutic reasons.'

'I didn't think so, doctor,' she murmured. 'And I've got the definite feeling this has nothing to do with keeping me warm.'

'Right. But—hell, Jessie, I——' He took a deep breath and let it out slowly. 'I'm sorry,' he said quickly, letting go of her and taking a step back. 'You're absolutely right.'

She looked at him in surprise. 'I am?'

'Of course you are. Hell, here you are, out in the middle of nowhere, alone with some guy who's helped you out some ...'

'You saved my life, Chad.'

'That's what I mean,' he said, almost angrily. 'Look, I don't want you to do anything out of gratitude or ...'

Anger blazed in her eyes. 'Do you think I would?' she demanded icily.

'Jesus, I am making a mess of this, aren't I? What I mean is, we're in a kind of artificial situation, Jessie, and I don't want ... I don't ... Hell, I just ...'

Suddenly, it was important to tell him she understood what he was trying to tell her. Something was happening between them, had been happening almost from the moment they'd met. She took a deep breath and raised her eyes to his.

'Are you telling me you're an old-fashioned gentleman, Chad O'Bryan? That would be fine, you know, because I'm a pretty old-fashioned type myself.'

'Yeah,' he said with a hesitant smile, 'that reference to Canton, Ohio gave me a shred of hope.'

Jessica laughed softly. 'I've got to tell you that you wouldn't get the chance to make any kind of move on me if we were in one of those places on Third Avenue.' A shadowed look of hurt darkened his hazel eyes and she shook her head. 'No, you don't understand,' she said quickly. 'I don't go to those places, Chad.' She shrugged her shoulders and smiled. 'You can take the girl out of Ohio, but you can't take Ohio out of the girl, I guess.'

He smiled at her. 'You had me going for a minute there, lady. I thought you were going to slice me to ribbons. So you don't bother with the hanging plants and the phoney stained glass, hmm?' She shook her head and he reached out and touched one of her dark curls. 'Well, then, where would I find you?'

'Depends on the weather,' she said, fighting against the desire to move so that his fingers would brush her skin. 'If it's raining, you might find me watching old movies at the Museum of Modern Art.'

'Old movies, hmm? Bogart? Bacall? That sort of thing?'

Jessica nodded her head. 'Exactly. I wouldn't have thought you'd like them, though.'

He laughed softly. 'I don't. I'm more a science fiction man myself. *Attack of the Killer Tomatoes* was a classic.'

Her eyes widened but she made no comment. Finally, she nodded her head again. 'Well, to each his own, I guess. What do you do when you're not watching gems like that?'

He grinned and ran his hand lightly along her cheek. 'In the city, you mean? Well, I like to go to the Museum of Natural History.'

'You'd find me across the park in the Metropolitan.'

'Yeah, that's a good museum, too, but the wildlife dioramas at the Museum of Natural History are great.'

Jessica nodded her head. 'I've seen those. They're very nice, but when I want to see animals, I go to the Bronx Zoo.'

'Do you? Well, then, that's where I'd have made my move on you.' Chad said happily. 'That's one of my favourite places.'

A sweet sense of relief flooded through her. Thank God, she thought, although she knew such jubilation was insane. After all, what did it matter whether they liked the same things or not? Still, she felt a goofy smile spread across her face.

'Me, too. I've taken I don't know how many pictures there. The African Plains, and the bear dens, and ...'

'You like animals?'

Jessica nodded. 'Oh, yes. Do you? I ...' She broke off and shook her head in embarrassment. 'I almost forgot that you were a wildlife biologist. Isn't that dumb?'

'I forget it, myself, most of the time,' he said. 'I was a cowboy for so long ...'

'Aha,' she laughed.

'Aha,' he repeated, grinning at her. 'My dad's a rancher. I used to work for him summers while I was in school ... So, OK, we'd have met at the Zoo. And I'd have made a move—something subtle, but definite—and you'd have said ...'

She shrugged her shoulders. 'Depends on what you'd tried on me, Dr O'Bryan,' she said teasingly. His hand closed around a lock of her hair and she cleared her throat. 'For instance, if you asked me to stop at the cafeteria and have a cup of coffee, I'd probably have said no.'

Chad lifted his eyebrows in surprise. 'Really?'

Jessica smiled. 'Have you ever tasted their coffee?'

He grinned. 'Suppose I asked you out to dinner?'

'I might say yes,' she said archly. 'Then again, I might say no.'

He sighed and shook his head. 'It's what I said before, Jessica Howard. You're a tough lady.' His hand moved into her hair and closed around the back of her head and an electric tremor ran through her. 'If you said no, I'd have no choice but to resort to my final tactic.'

Her heart gave a sudden thud. 'And what would that be?'

He smiled and moved nearer to her. 'I'd have moved

up close to you while you were taking your pictures ...'

'I'd have thought you would have been concentrating on watching the animals, Dr O'Bryan.'

His hand slid to her shoulder. 'Observation of the species is a basic scientific necessity.'

'Did anybody ever tell you you've got a pretty good big city technique, cowboy?'

'I don't know what you mean, Jessie,' he said innocently. 'I'm just trying to be helpful. I know lots about species behaviour, you see ...'

'Yes,' she said, 'I'll bet you do.' His arms closed around her. She could feel the hard length of his body pressing lightly against hers, feel the heat of him burning through the layers of clothing. She looked into his eyes and saw the sudden gleam of topaz fire. Her throat became dry; all the teasing banter was gone. A minute ago, the thought of his kiss had seemed an exciting possibility. Now, suddenly, it was an over-whelming one. 'Chad,' she whispered, 'don't ...'

'You don't mean that, Jessie,' he murmured. 'I can see what you want in your eyes.'

She put her hands on his chest; she could feel the rapid thud of his heart and she knew it matched the racing beat of her own.

'I don't know what I want,' she whispered. 'We only just met ...'

Chad's arms tightened around her. 'Hell, we've lived a lifetime since we met. People who've known each other for weeks don't know each other as well as we do.'

She nodded her head. 'Yes, yes, I know that, but ...' She took a shuddering breath. How could she explain? He was right about what she wanted; even when she'd told herself she despised him, there had been a spark between them just waiting to flame into passion. But everything about the past couple of days had been outside the realm of reality—and reality was what would happen in five or six days when they got out of these mountains. He would go back to his world and she would go back to hers and all this would be a bitter sweet memory. 'I can't,' she said. 'I can't.'

Their eyes met; she waited in silence, knowing that if he kissed her, it would be impossible to deny the need stirring within her, and then he let out his breath.

'You're right, Jessie,' he said, running his thumb lightly along her cheek. 'I promised you a fire and dinner, and I haven't delivered on either one. And I want to take a look at your ankle.' His hands slid along her back and then fell to his sides. 'So,' he said with forced lightness, 'are you ready for Beans O'Bryan?'

'I . . . thank you,' she murmured.

He smiled at her. 'For what? You haven't tasted my Cherries Jubilee yet.'

She laughed softly. 'I thought it was Peach Melba.'

He grinned as he knelt in front of the fireplace. 'Does it matter? I promise, after a few days with me, your tastes will never be the same again.'

Yes, she thought, watching him in silence, that was a real possibility.

CHAPTER EIGHT

CHAD lifted an ancient cast iron skillet from the fireplace and set it on the table with a flourish.

'Just wait until you taste this, Jessie. I think you'll agree the chef's outdone himself.'

'The chef wouldn't be a bit prejudiced, would he?' Jessica sank into the chair opposite him and sniffed the steam rising from the skillet. 'No matter what you say, it looks like beans to me.'

'Come on, woman,' he said, holding out a spoonful of the stuff to her, 'where's your sense of adventure? Try some.'

Dutifully, she did as he asked and then she sighed. 'So much for the answer to the age-old riddle—what looks like beans, smells like beans, and tastes like beans?'

'You're hurting the chef's feelings, Jess.'

She smiled at him as she dug her spoon into the skillet. 'Forgive me. These are lunch beans as opposed to dinner beans or breakfast beans.'

'These are Beans du Jour. The ones last night were Beans de la Maison and that batch this morning were an old O'Bryan speciality—Beans Ranchero.'

Jessica swallowed a mouthful of the brownish concoction and nodded wisely. 'I see. And what, pray tell, was the difference between them?'

Chad shrugged modestly. 'A dollop of ketchup, some molasses from that jug we found in the general store, and a lot of imagination.'

Jessica smiled as she broke off a piece of cold bannock. 'Three cheers for the general store,' she said, dipping the bannock into the beans. 'And three more for whoever taught you to cook. Don't let it go to your head, doctor, but this trail bread's not bad.'

'Just wait until tonight when you finally taste what I can do with rainbow trout.' He spooned up a mouthful of beans and chewed them carefully. 'Not bad, if I say so myself. My dad would be proud of me.'

'Was he the one who taught you to cook? Remind me to drop him a note of thanks when we get out of here.'

'It was self-preservation on his part. Ranch cooks used to come and go; I guess he got tired of being the back-up cook for the two of us and the hands. He taught me to lasso a calf and make stew at about the same time. By the time I was ten, I could find my way around a kitchen as easily as around a corral.'

'It must be awful to lose your mother when you're little.'

Chad shrugged his shoulders. 'I don't remember any other kind of life,' he said truthfully. 'The only time it made things rough was when I decided I wanted to specialise in wildlife biology. It meant spending a lot of time in the natural habitat of whatever species you're studying—and I felt kind of guilty about leaving my father alone.'

'But?'

'But it worked out. He met my stepmother about then. Not that he'd have said anything to me ... I guess it's rough for a parent when a kid leaves home.'

Jessica sighed as she dipped a piece of bannock into the beans. 'I know what you mean. When I said I was moving to New York, you'd have thought the end of the world had arrived.'

'Well, it had,' Chad laughed. 'I agree there. Why on earth would anyone want to live there?'

'That's exactly what my folks said. But New York's

the hub of everything. Well, I guess Chicago was closer, but all my life I dreamed about Manhattan—you know, having a loft in Soho and having a show of my photos at a Greenwich Village gallery.'

"'If you can make it there, you can make it anywhere,'" he said. 'Is that it?'

'Well, it's the truth, isn't it?'

Chad shrugged his shoulders. 'Maybe. I guess it depends on what you want out of life. I just can't picture you spending the rest of yours photographing under-nourished models wearing stuff that looks like Hallow-een costumes.'

For an instant, Jessica's eyes narrowed and then she let out a sighing breath. 'You know something? I can't picture it either.'

Chad grinned as he mopped up the last of the beans with a piece of bannock. 'For a minute there, I thought I was going to get another lecture about the fashion business.'

'Oh, I'm not knocking it. After all, this job's been interesting. I've travelled to some great places ...'

'Oh yeah,' he laughed, 'that must be great!'

She grinned at him and then licked her spoon clean. 'Well, the flying part isn't, but I manage. And I've gotten to watch some pretty good photographers at work. I've learned more in the past couple of years than I could have in any photography course.' She tilted her head to one side and gave Chad an appraising look. 'You know what would be great?'

'Yeah,' he grinned. 'Something other than beans for lunch.'

Jessica laughed and pushed her plate away. 'I was thinking that maybe you could give me some pointers about animal photography. I got some great shots at the Bronx Zoo but I know I missed some things.'

'Shots of what? The Children's Zoo? The seals?'

She shook her head. 'They've been done to death. What I got interested in was this litter of wolf cubs ... Do you know where the wolf enclosure is? Why are you looking at me like that?'

'I can't believe it, Jessie. We damned well should have met, if you were taking pictures of those little guys. That's my speciality. Wolf studies, I mean. I've got a theory about pack structure ...'

'Are you telling me you study wolves at the Bronx Zoo?'

'I study wolves where they live, Jess—in Alaska and Michigan and Canada. But I did a paper on the effect of captivity on breeding habits ... Listen, as soon as the weather clears, I'd be delighted to give you some ideas on animal photography,' he said eagerly. 'Matter of fact, I noticed some deer tracks yesterday when I followed the main street of Coleman's Creek out of town. Did I tell you it ends at a railroad spur? Not that I was surprised— it was pretty much what I expected.'

'You mean train tracks?' Jessica's face lit with excitement. 'Why didn't you say something, Chad? There's a way out, then.'

He shook his head. 'Sorry, Jess. The tracks end under what looks like a billion tons of earth and rock. There must have been one hell of a slide here some time after the town was abandoned.'

'I see,' she said quietly. She put down her spoon and looked across the table at him. 'Chad, are we trapped here?' she asked quietly. 'We haven't talked about it, but you know my ankle's fine now and you still haven't said anything about moving on.'

'I keep hoping for a break in the weather. But each time it stops snowing, the clouds build up over the mountain and a new front moves in. There's no way of telling how much snow's going to fall, Jessie, and if we were on the mountain when a heavy storm hit . . .' He reached for her hand and covered it with his. 'At least here we have shelter and food and firewood.'

'Yes, but . . . well, no matter how we joke, the beans won't last for ever. And that fireplace consumes more dead branches than any human being could collect once the weather gets colder. And it will get colder, won't it?'

'Yeah, a little,' he said, thinking of the sub-zero winters in these mountains and the endless snow. 'But if hermits can manage, so can we. The creek's full of fish and I can set snares for rabbits and squirrels, and tell you they're sirloin steaks and veal scallops . . .' She gave him a hesitant smile and his hand tightened on hers. 'We'll be fine, Jess. I promise.'

She sighed and touched her finger to a piece of bannock. 'I've never felt so . . . so cut off from the world. I'm just grateful my folks are on vacation. Imagine how awful it would be if they were worrying about me.' A furrow appeared between her eyes as she looked at Chad. 'You really don't think they could have heard about the crash?'

He shook his head. 'When a light plane goes down with two people on board, it doesn't make much more than the local papers.'

'But there'll still be search parties looking for us, won't there?'

'Of course,' he said with more enthusiasm than he felt. His eyes searched hers. 'Hey,' he said lightly, 'is this what an all-bean diet leads to?' A smile flitted across her face and quickly vanished. 'Or is it nicotine withdrawal that caused this serious case of the blahs?'

To his relief, her smile broadened. 'I've been meaning to bring that up,' she said. 'If you're so great at survival techniques, how come you haven't snared me a pack of cigarettes?'

'And pollute this clean mountain air? Not on your life.'

She laughed and the tension flowed out of her face. 'You know, cowboy, if I had to find myself stranded like this, I'm glad it's with you.'

'I was just thinking the same thing, Jessie. There's nobody I'd rather be here with.'

The laughter was gone in an instant, chased away by the caressing sound in Chad's voice. Jessica's eyes lifted to his; the message she saw in their hazel depths made the breath catch in her throat.

'Jessie . . .'

She pulled her hand free of his and got to her feet, almost stumbling as she pushed her chair back from the table. The air between them was suddenly thick with tension as it had been all too often in the past couple of days. She told herself she knew the reason for it. After all, they were trapped in an enforced intimacy that had intensified normal feelings and reactions. That was all it was. That was all it could be . . . She heard him push away from the table and she moved quickly towards the fireplace.

'Jessie,' he said again.

'I mean, if I had to pick a man to be lost in the wilderness with,' she said in a brightly pitched voice, 'I'd certainly pick someone like you. Who else would know so much about survival? Who else would have known about Coleman's Creek? Who else would . . .'

'Damn it, Jessie,' he said, 'that's not what I meant.'

'I'll always be grateful to you,' she said, fighting against the desire to turn and wrap her arms around him. 'Always.'

Her voice was polite and impersonal, and it brought

him to a dead stop. Damn it, O'Bryan, he told himself, why don't you stop misreading the signs? She's made it clear enough. Gratitude is what she feels, that's all. And it's just as well. The last thing you need is to let this city woman get under your skin.

The stool clattered as he pushed it aside. 'I'm going down to the creek,' he said. 'It may take a while to catch our dinner.'

Jessica turned at the sound of his voice. His words were simple, but there was a rawness to them that made her want to reach out to him.

'Chad?' she said quickly. He turned towards her and she hesitated. 'I . . . I'm really looking forward to those trout,' she said finally.

'Great,' he mumbled, pulling on his jacket.

'Yes,' she said, eager to dissipate the sudden tension in the cabin, 'in fact, if you catch some, I'll do the cooking tonight.' She smiled shyly. 'Of course, you'll have to use your imagination for the butter and almonds.'

'Butter and almonds?' he repeated. Jessica nodded her head and smiled again. Damn, he thought, it didn't take much to make her happy. It was impossible not to return her smile. In fact, he felt as if he'd handed her a dozen long-stemmed roses. 'Are we talking about trout almondine?'

'We are, indeed,' she said happily, watching the lines ease from around his mouth. 'I happen to be a pretty terrific gourmet cook.'

'Really?' She nodded her head and he smiled. 'Well, then, maybe you can do something to improve those beans.'

'The key word there was "gourmet",' she laughed. 'I'm not much when it comes to everyday stuff.'

'Don't tell me you eat trout almondine every night.'

'Mostly, I eat out. Between my job and photography

courses, I'm too tired to potter in the kitchen.'

Chad nodded. 'I should have figured that. There must be guys lined up ten deep outside your door, fighting for the chance to take you to dinner.'

'No,' she said, so quickly that she startled both of them. 'I mean, I usually stop in this little place near my apartment and read a book while I eat.'

Chad's eyes met hers. 'Really? What's the matter with those New York guys, anyway?'

She smiled slowly. 'Nothing, I guess. I—I just haven't found anybody who . . .' Her words trailed off and finally she cleared her throat. 'What about you?' she asked. 'Is there—is there somebody special who treats you to home-cooked meals when you get back from the snowy wastes of Alaska?'

'No,' he said simply, 'there's nobody.' They looked at each other and then he smiled. 'And you'd better not let an Alaskan hear you say that. It's not the end of the world, you know.'

'It is, to me. Endless snow and Eskimos . . .'

'But it's not like that, Jessie,' he said quickly. 'Parts of it are primitive, yes, but there are towns and cities.'

'New York is a city,' she answered. 'Anything else is an impostor.'

Damn, but she sounded smug, he thought. For some reason, her reaction irritated him and he scowled. 'Have you ever tried living any place else?'

'I come from Canton, Ohio, remember? No other place has New York's facilities or its opportunities.'

'Or its pollution or its crime rate or its crowds.'

'There's not a city in the world that doesn't have those things.'

Chad nodded his head. 'Exactly!'

God, she thought, just listen to him! The single word was so . . . so all-knowing, so pompously self-assured. An inexplicable anger grew within her. 'Well, so much for all the cities of the world,' she said carefully. 'They're nice places to visit but you wouldn't want to live in one, right?'

'If you understood my work, Jessie, you'd realise that I have to be in the field. I'm not a lab man. That's not my thing . . .'

'Am I right?' she demanded.

He shrugged his shoulders. 'Yeah, I guess you are.'

Well, she thought, what had she expected? She poured some hot water into the skillet. 'I thought you were going to catch some trout,' she said. 'It's getting late, isn't it?'

Chad watched as Jessica scrubbed furiously at the skillet with a rag and then he picked up his backpack and slipped his arms through its straps. 'I'm going now,' he said gruffly. 'I'll be back as soon as I can. Remember to keep that fire built up.'

'Don't worry about a thing,' she said coolly. 'Take your time.'

The door slammed shut and her shoulders slumped. What a senseless argument! Had she expected him to say, 'I'm going to change my whole life, now that I've met you, Jessie? If you're in New York, I will be, too.'

'Damn!' she said softly, wiping her hands on her jeans. Maybe this was cabin fever, for real. If only they could get out of here. If only they hadn't been trapped by a snowstorm . . . Of course, Chad didn't call it that. In fact, he'd laughed at her when she made the pronouncement the day before.

'This isn't a snowstorm, Jess,' he'd said, coming to stand beside her in the open doorway. 'That's only about five inches of snow out there.'

'You're right,' she'd agreed solemnly, staring at the blowing snow. 'It's not a storm, it's a blizzard.'

He smiled and slipped his arm lightly around her shoulders. 'Maybe in New York. Here, it's nothing but a dusting. Beautiful, isn't it?'

She nodded, trying to ignore the tingling sensation that sprang up where his arm touched her. 'That ridge looks as if someone sprinkled it with sugar. I can hardly wait to get outside with my camera. I want to walk up to the top.'

'You won't have time.'

'Sure I will. It's early—we have lots of daylight left.'

He shook his head. 'You can't be out more than ten minutes, Jessie.'

'Come on, Chad, what are you talking about? It'll take me that long just to get to the ridge.'

'Ten minutes,' he repeated. 'If you don't agree to that, you can't go out at all.'

She stepped back and tilted her head to one side. 'Are you kidding me?'

'You can't go out for long wearing sneakers. And you haven't got enough warm clothing.'

'I have, Chad. I look like a gypsy in all these layers but I'm warm ...'

'I don't want you to get cold and wet, Jess.'

'For goodness' sake, you sound like my mother,' she laughed. 'I've had chills before and survived them. Don't worry.'

'Ten minutes,' he ordered. 'That's it.'

She tossed her head and grabbed her sweater from the table. 'You're letting your title go to your head, doctor. You're not a medical man, you know.'

'Ten minutes,' he repeated. 'Have you got that?'

'Excuse me,' she said politely. 'Would you just step aside?'

Chad slammed the door and leaned his back against it, arms crossed in front of his chest. 'I didn't hear your answer, Jessie,' he said softly.

'That's because I didn't give you one,' she said. 'Now, I'm going out.'

'Sure,' he said easily. 'You can do whatever you like.'

Her eyes narrowed. 'Well, then . . .'

'Once you get past me.'

'Come on, Chad.'

'Come on, Jessie. All you have to do is open this door.'

What a stupid quarrel this was, she thought. Everything he'd said made sense: the snow was deep and it would be stupid to get wet and chilled to the bone, especially since they had nothing more therapeutic than a handful of aspirin. Her eyes met his and she drew in her breath. There was something about his narrowed eyes and lazy smile that made her pulse beat quicken, something that made her want to defy him, to push him past the bonds of propriety . . .

'Step aside,' she said, reaching for the doorknob. His hand shot out and curled around her wrist. A thrill of excitement raced through her. 'Let go of me,' she said. 'I can take care of myself.'

'You're not behaving as if you can.'

'What gives you the right . . .'

'I care about you,' he said, his voice rough with anger. 'That gives me the right. Damn it, Jessie, will you listen?'

'No,' she said, 'no, I won't.'

'You will, even if I have to make you!'

The thrill coursed through her again. 'That's right,' she said, trying to twist free of him. 'Prove how big and tough you are. I forgot you were an expert in western macho. I forgot . . .'

She was trying to pull free of his hand. In their silent struggle, he drew her towards him and her body pressed against his. Suddenly they were both still, shocked into immobility by the unexpected, electric contact, and then his arms closed around her and his mouth captured hers. Her hands rose between them, pushing ineffectually against his chest; then, with a speed that took her breath away, Jessica felt herself sinking into his embrace, just as she had the other times he'd taken her in his arms, only this time she wanted the feeling to go on for ever. It was only when she felt his arms tightening around her like bands of steel, only when her lips parted in urgent response to the increasing demand of his, that she suddenly knew she had to pull free of his embrace if she were to keep from falling into a velvet abyss from which there might be no return. It took all her strength to pull her mouth from his. The sound of their ragged breathing filled the small room; she could hear the pounding of her blood in her ears.

'That wasn't fair,' she whispered.

'You're right,' he answered, running his hand along her cheek. 'It wasn't meant to be.'

She had turned away then, upset as much by the knowledge that he had deliberately engineered what had happened as by her reaction to it. Chad hadn't stopped her as she slipped past him. Instead, he'd followed her down the snowy main street of the ghost town, watching in silence as she snapped off a roll of film. The cold air and blowing snow had cleared her head, but soon her fingers and toes felt numb and she'd glanced at her watch.

'I've got three minutes to spare,' she'd said. 'But I'm going inside now.'

He had smiled politely. 'Good idea.'

They'd spent the rest of the afternoon at a companionable distance, sitting in front of the fire, playing a lopsided game of poker with a mouse-nibbled deck of cards that was missing a queen of hearts and an eight of clubs. Neither of them had referred to the swift magic of their kiss. But Jessica hadn't forgotten it; she hadn't slept well last night and she knew Chad hadn't, either. The darkness in the little cabin had been filled with their awareness of each other. She'd heard Chad arrange and rearrange his tarpaulin on the floor near the fireplace. She'd been awake when he slipped quietly outside, awake still when he'd come back into the little cabin a long while later ...

The skillet fell from her hand and clattered to the floor. She bent and picked it up, scratching absently at a speck of dried beans on the handle. How quickly things change, she thought. A few days ago, she'd have shuddered at the sight of a less than clean dish or pan. A few days ago ...

Something banged loudly against the cabin window. Jessica spun around and looked across the room, heart pounding. The hermit? she wondered. Chad had said he was long gone, but still ...

She laughed shakily. It had been a branch, she realised, brought down from the lodgepole pine that stood like a sentinel just outside the cabin. The weight of the snow must have broken it off. There was a loud, snapping sound: another branch, she thought, and then, suddenly, there was a roaring noise in the chimney. She leaped backwards as a deluge of snow and ash tumbled into the hearth, smothering the fire and filling the cabin with sooty smoke. Dear Lord, she thought, as dry coughs racked her throat, what had happened? Quickly, she grabbed her sweater and wrenched open the door.

The snow crunched sharply underfoot as she stepped outside. A large pine branch lay on the roof; she could see at a glance what had happened. The snow had broken a heavy branch and it had fallen on the chimney. Only a couple of bricks had been knocked off the top, but the branch had disgorged its snowy cargo down the chimney. Jessica ducked back into the smoky cabin and stalked to the fireplace.

What a mess! She squatted before the hearth and stared at the tumble of snow and wood. The cabin was chilling already; without the blazing fire, the cold air that found its way through the chinks in the logs had free reign in the little room. Well, she thought, there was nothing to do but clear the hearth and rebuild the fire. And the sooner she got to work, the better.

By the time she had finished, her arms and back were fierce knots of pain. But the hearth was clean; she had emptied it of ashes, wet wood and snow and now it awaited the laying of a fresh fire. That should do it, she thought, arranging the last bit of kindling and wood. And just in time; even with all the heavy work she'd been doing, she was beginning to feel the cold. Jessica got to her feet and reached to the table behind her for the matches. She could hardly wait for the first tiny leap of flame, the first curl of smoke ...

'Damn!' she said aloud, turning towards the table. Where were the matches? In her pockets, perhaps? No, not there. On the floor, then? 'Damn,' she said again. That was where they were, all right ... soaked, limp, and useless as they lay in a melted puddle of snow. She picked them up and tossed them aside. There had to be another book of matches somewhere. But a methodical check of all their supplies and clothing turned up nothing. Well, at least she knew where the balance of their precious hoard of matches was, she thought, repressing a shiver as the cold knifed into the little cabin. They were in a waterproof container in Chad's backpack—and the backpack was at the creek with its owner.

She pulled on her last remaining sweater and buttoned it. Its warmth was fleeting and within seconds, she was shivering. Keep the fire built up, Chad had said, and now they didn't even have a fire. She clapped her icy hands together and two-stepped around the room like a demented ballerina. By the time he got back, she'd be a lump of frozen flesh. And he'd be chilled to the bone after all this time down at the creek, expecting to be greeted by a warm, roaring fire . . .

Well, there was a simple solution. The creek was barely a five-minute walk away. Chad had described its location to her the first day. She hadn't been there—the first few days, her ankle had hurt too much. She hadn't dared suggest it yesterday, not after their run-in about her getting sick if she got wet and cold . . . Ten minutes, he'd said, she could be outside for ten minutes and no longer, which meant he couldn't very well scold her for going after the matches. The whole thing would take no more than that. And besides, she told herself, marching towards the door, what choice did she really have? She could either go out there and freeze her nose off, or sit here and freeze her bottom off.

She hesitated as she closed the door behind her. What had he said that first night? A rule of survival, he'd called it. Know where you've been, know where you are, know where you're going. And she knew all three. The creek was due east of the cabin, and there were Chad's tracks. All she had to do was follow them. It was cold, of course, but the kiss of the sun was pleasant on her face. Her ragtag gypsy outfit seemed warm enough, although she could feel the occasional sharp bite of the wind through it. The snow crunched loudly under her feet as she walked along Main Street.

Lord, it was so quiet! The sagging doors and windows of the empty ghost town seemed to watch her accusingly as she trudged through the snow. Chad's footsteps stretched ahead like signposts along a highway. She hunched down into her sweater, picturing his reaction to her arrival at the creek. He'd be surprised, that was for sure. He might even be annoyed, but only until she explained what had happened. Would he want to move to another cabin? No, she thought, he'd picked this one because its roof and walls were intact, as was its door and both its old glass windows. The chimney was still functional, as far as she could tell. And there didn't seem to be any other branches hanging over the roof.

Jessica glanced up at the sky and a shudder ran through her. There was a cloud moving over the sun and without its brightness, the temperature seemed to have dropped ten degrees. Where was that creek, anyway? Five minutes east, Chad had said, but she'd left the town behind at least that long ago and there wasn't any sign of a creek or a pond or anything larger than the icy puddles she kept stepping over and around. And into, she thought with a grimace. It had become impossible to follow his footsteps; the wind had sculpted the snow into curves and ridges and obliterated them.

She halted and tucked her cold hands into her armpits. No wonder he'd warned her about staying outside more than ten minutes; her feet were like ice and her fingers felt as if they were falling off. Had he . . . could he have said the creek was west of the cabin? She remembered that he'd pointed towards a ridge line, and she'd noticed how rounded it was. Shivering, she glanced behind her at the soft lines of the mountains to the west.

'OK, dummy,' she said with a sigh, 'it looks as if you walked in the wrong direction. But you still know where you are and where you've been. As for where you're going, it had better be back towards the cabin.'

She took a deep breath and started back the way she'd

come, surprised at how tired and out of breath she felt. But the snow made walking difficult, especially now that her sneakers were soaked. Her spirits lifted as she spotted the cabin dead ahead. For an instant, she was tempted to go inside and simply wait for Chad to return. But then she thought about how chilled and wet she was, and the more she thought about it, the less intelligent it seemed to sit for who knew how long in the freezing cold when she could find the cowboy, get the extra matches and start a warm fire. 'Keep moving, Jessie,' she said aloud, trudging past the cabin. 'You're almost there now.'

But she wasn't. Her footsteps lagged; she stopped and stared around her. The cabin was behind her and out of view and there still wasn't anything resembling a creek in sight. She shifted her feet uncomfortably; they felt leaden and numb. She had a fleeting image of the heavy wool coat hanging in her cupboard back in New York. Boy, she could certainly use it now, she thought, wrapping her arms around herself. She'd never felt this cold, not in her whole life. Her face felt as if it might crack if she touched it, and the chill wind seemed to cut through her layered sweaters as if they weren't even there. But she couldn't give up now; she was probably only a few hundred yards from the creek. Maybe she'd gotten a bit off course. Maybe that hill to the right was the one she should be heading towards . . .

'Last try, Jessie,' she said aloud, trudging off again. 'If you don't find it this time, give it up.'

It made sense, she thought, digging her cold hands into her jean pockets. Even someone who did all her walking on the streets of New York knew it was dumb to wander around in the woods alone. Not that this was the woods, exactly. This was almost a meadow—there were trees, but not too many, and . . .

'Whoops!' Jessica swore under her breath. She was

tripping over her own feet. Well, why not? For one thing, the ankle she'd twisted days before had begun to hurt again. And it was getting hard to see; the sky was getting greyer all the time. The sun was almost hidden behind the mountains—it was a ball of glowing orange, but she was too cold to appreciate it at the moment. And there was definitely no creek in this direction either, she thought suddenly, coming to a halt. There was nothing but snow-covered landscape ahead, stretching as far as she could see ...

'That's it, kid. Back you go,' she said aloud, turning and trudging across the valley. There was a tiny knot of fear in her chest and she fought it back. Where was that damned cabin? She couldn't see it, not anywhere, not ahead or to the side or ...

Don't panic, she thought. Take it easy. Take some deep breaths. Great idea. But you couldn't take deep breaths when you were panting and your lungs ached from the icy air. OK, then, concentrate on something. Think about explaining all this to Chad. He'd probably be at the cabin by the time she got there and he'd have a few choice things to say. But she hadn't violated his rule of survival—she knew where she was. Obviously, it was the cabin that had got lost.

She laughed aloud at the thought. God, but that was funny! She'd have to remember that line. She could tell that to Chad when he said ... when he said ... When he said what? Wasn't that crazy? She had been thinking about something, and it had just slipped away from her. Of course it was crazy ...

Her footsteps slowed. Where had that stand of pines come from? Coleman's Creek was situated among lodgepole pines, not these gnarled, twisted trees. Chad had pointed out that the lodgepoles were straight and tall, he'd told her that was why they'd been given the name, because the Indians used to cut them down and use them to construct their lodges.

A gust of wind sighed through the trees, tumbling a dusting of snow from the branches overhead. It landed lightly on her shoulders. She raised her hand to brush it off but her fingers didn't seem to want to obey. She spread her hand before her face and stared at it. How could those fingers be hers? They didn't feel like hers—they felt thick and clumsy. She smiled. Wasn't it remarkable, though? Her hands didn't feel cold any more. No part of her did, now that she thought about it. She laughed softly. Wait until she got back to the cabin and told Chad how foolish his warnings had been. The wet and the cold wouldn't make you sick. All you had to do was adjust to the weather. If only she weren't so damned tired.

Night was coming on, but that was no problem. The cabin was out there somewhere; she'd taken a wrong turn or made a wrong step or something. All she had to do was keep walking towards the rounded mountain . . . She frowned and cocked her head to the side. Was that right? No, she thought, no, the rounded mountain was where the creek had been. But the creek hadn't been anywhere. Neither had the cabin. Well, she'd find the cabin and if not the cabin, then she'd find the creek and it didn't really matter which she found first, did it?

She laughed again. It was a riddle. Did the creek come first or did the cabin? It was like the chicken and the . . . the chicken and the . . . the something . . . It didn't really matter. She felt so good, so relaxed—like the way she'd felt at her high school graduation party, light and floaty and giggly. That was the time two of the guys had spiked the punch and no one had known anything about it until the next day when everybody had been sick to their stomachs and then she remembered thinking, so that's what it is to be drunk ...

'Whoops!' Her feet slipped out from under her and she landed on her rump. Her laughter died suddenly and tears filled her eyes. She was so clumsy. It was terrible to be like that. And she was so tired ... At least it was comfortable sitting here. Maybe she'd just lie down and rest for a while.

'Jessie ... Jessie ...'

Chad's voice floated to her on the sighing wind. For a second, she struggled to open her eyes and answer, and then she frowned and shook her head. No, she thought, he'd be angry because she'd made a mess of the rules. You were supposed to know something but she couldn't remember what it was ...

'Jessica, where are you? Please, Jessie, answer me.'

She whimpered softly. She wanted to go to him, even if he scolded her, even if he told her she'd been dumb. She wanted to throw herself into his arms and tell him ... tell him ...

'Jessie? Oh, God, Jessie ...'

A shadowy figure knelt beside her. She narrowed her eyes and tried to concentrate on the figure's face, but it took so much effort.

'Chad?' she whispered.

'Thank God,' he murmured hoarsely, lifting her into his arms. He held her against his heart for an instant and then touched his mouth to hers. Fear caught at his gut. Her skin was cool, her lips tinged with blue. There was a strange, almost unearthly quality about her ...

Hypothermia, he thought. He had seen it once before, in Alaska. One of the men he was working with had fallen into an icy stream. They'd pulled him out before he drowned, but not before his internal temperature had dropped rapidly. A couple of minutes later, the poor bastard was acting like a drunk. He could barely string three words together or stand up, much less walk back to their Land Rover. And they'd almost lost him, Chad remembered, while fear knifed through him again. It had been touch and go.

His arms tightened around Jessica and he rose to his feet. 'You'll be fine, Jessie,' he said fiercely. 'I swear it, love, I swear it.'

Whispering assurances as much to himself as to her, he started towards the cabin at a trot, slipping and stumbling in the drifting snow. Slow down, O'Bryan, he told himself, slow down, or neither one of you will get there.

'You'll be fine, Jessie,' he said again, almost crooning the words into her ear.

She made a sound midway between a sob and a laugh. 'I am fine,' she mumbled, her voice thick and furry. 'You're not the only wilfer—wilter—wiln'ness expert, Doctor.'

'Where the hell were you going?' he demanded, even though he knew the question was meaningless to her, that she was past logical thought and reason.

'Don't be ...'

He bent his head to hers. 'What is it, love? I couldn't hear ...'

'Don' be angry,' she whispered drunkenly. 'I was ... I was looking for you. The cabin ...' She fought to remember what had been so important about the cabin, what she'd set out to tell him, but it was impossible.

'Yes, love, yes,' he whispered, 'we're at the cabin now.'

He kicked open the door and stepped into the little room. It was chilled and damp. There was no fire in the fireplace, only a stacked batch of fresh wood and kindling. Chad deposited Jessica tenderly before it and covered her with the motley assortment of torn blankets and musty scraps of fabric they'd collected from the other cabins. She was so pale, so cold . . .

It took less than a minute for him to dig out the matches from his pack and start a fire, and then he went back to her. Her eyes were closed and her breathing shallow. A terror unlike any he'd ever known filled him. With trembling fingers, he began to ease the cold, wet clothing from her limp body.

CHAPTER NINE

CHAD brushed a tendril of hair off Jessica's forehead and she sighed in her sleep and turned away from his hand. It was such a natural, simple action that it made him smile. Hell, he thought, a couple of hours ago he'd been afraid she'd never do anything that normal again. She'd been like a rag doll in his arms, limp and senseless while he took off her wet clothing and then dried her chilled body. Carefully, fearful she might choke, he'd spoon-fed her some warm bark and berry tea, constantly talking to her, urging her to live, scolding her for her having left the cabin and then telling her it was his fault, that he should have warned her about hypothermia, even though he knew she couldn't hear him. But talking had kept him sane; he hadn't stopped until the glow began to return to her skin and she fell into a deep sleep, not into the coma that would have led to death. 'Thank you,' he had whispered, and then he'd cradled her in his arms and watched her as she slept.

Another storm had moved in during the past couple of hours. He could hear the high-pitched howl of the wind as it rushed through the trees, but it was warm and comfortable in the cabin. Chad yawned and burrowed deeper into the tangle of blankets. Just a half-hour's nap, he thought, that was all he needed. Then he'd see if it was time to put another log on the fire and maybe heat some more tea for Jessie. She might be awake by then . . . Jesus, he thought, a smile flickering across his face, he could just imagine her reaction to things when she woke up. Well, he'd explain the second she opened her eyes.

He was just too tired to think about it now . . .

Asleep yet not asleep, suspended half-way between dreams and reality, Jessica struggled towards a dim light glowing somewhere above her. She hated the sensation; it was the way she'd felt when she was ten and she'd had to have a tooth pulled and the dentist had sent her to a place where they put a needle into her arm. You'll fall asleep, the nurse had said, but she hadn't fallen asleep, she'd plunged into an abyss and then, the next thing she knew, she was drifting through time, looking down on herself as she lay on a couch in the recovery room, her body waiting for her mind and soul to re-enter it.

She fought against the image of the dental surgery. There was no smell of antiseptic, there was just a pleasant blend of scents. Woodsmoke, she thought, woodsmoke . . .

Her eyes snapped open. Of course she could smell woodsmoke. She was in the cabin at Coleman's Creek and . . . had she fallen asleep in front of the fireplace? Yes, she must have. She was in a soft cocoon of blankets and she was wonderfully warm; a silken heat seemed to surround her. She stretched lazily, luxuriating in the warmth. Her skin felt heated, ablaze . . .

Her breath caught in her throat. She was sleeping beside Chad. No, that didn't half describe it. Chad was lying on his back and she was cradled in his arms, her head nestled on his shoulder, both of them warm and cosy under what seemed like every blanket in the cabin. The only thing that separated their bodies was a thin scrap of blanket that had got tangled between them. But it was hardly a barrier; she could feel the ridge of his ribcage and the hard muscles of his stomach pressing against her. And she was aware of every heated inch of his body from ankle to thigh to . . .

No, she thought, it was impossible. . . Her heartbeat

skidded erratically. Under the pile of blankets, she was as naked as a baby. And Chad ... even the worn blanket caught between them couldn't hide the fact that he was as naked as she was. She could feel the satiny hardness of his bare flesh under her cheek, see his chest, golden in the flickering firelight ...

My God, she thought, how ...? And when? She closed her eyes, willing the return of memory, but there was nothing, nothing ... Only an image of snow and trees, a fleeting remembrance of freezing cold and wet. Please, she thought, taking a ragged breath, please, there had to be more. She fought against the grey emptiness until finally there was a sudden rush of unsettling, half-formed images and sensations: the comforting feel of Chad's arms and the sound of his voice and his whispered words ... and then oblivion. But something had happened between then and now, something that had left her nude and in his arms.

An inky blackness filled the little cabin. She knew it must be two or three in the morning; the past nights in the wilderness had taught her that the hours just past midnight were the deepest part of the night. Only the flickering of the fire pierced the dark. She had a sudden picture of the flames in the hearth extinguished under the punishing burden of the snow. Yes, she remembered now—the falling branch, the limp matches ... She'd gone to find Chad, hadn't she? And she must have succeeded; otherwise, the cabin would be cold and dark. With effort, she could recall going out into the snow but everything after that was wrapped in a milky haze ... There was a vague memory of bone chilling cold and then ... and then Chad lifting her into his arms and bringing her back to the cabin and then the heat of his hands and his body ...

She froze as he stirred and murmured something

unintelligible. After a heart-stopping instant, his arm tightened around her and he drew her against him. She held her breath until he was still again. Then, with deliberate caution, she lifted her head, tilting it back until she could glimpse his face. Thank God, she thought, he was still asleep, his lashes lying against his bristled cheeks like dark smudges. How could she face him? She couldn't even remember what had happened. And that was impossible. Of course it was impossible. The times he had kissed her had left her trembling, wanting him with a need that frightened her. Surely his lovemaking would have seared her soul. Then why couldn't she remember?

He stirred again and moved against her. She closed her eyes, almost overcome by sensation. How many times had she thought about being in his arms like this? She longed to stay right where she was, safe and secure and warm.

Get moving, Jessie, she thought quickly. Do it now, while you can. Get away from the feel of his body, the sweet scent of his breath, the steadying beat of his heart. Slowly, carefully, she began to ease herself away from him. But not carefully enough, she thought, as he awoke with the rapidity of a sleeping tiger.

'Well, now,' he said softly. 'Welcome back, Jessie.'

She closed her eyes in despair. 'Chad?' she said stupidly.

He chuckled softly. 'Who did you expect?'

She twisted her fingers in the thin blanket caught between them, clutching it to her.

'I . . . I must have slept for hours.'

'Yeah, you did.' His arm tightened around her and he cleared his throat. 'You gave me quite a scare.'

She ran her tongue across her lips and tugged uselessly at the blanket, as if that would change it into a suit of armour, or at least something longer and wider and thicker. Now was hardly the time to tell him she hadn't the faintest idea of what he was talking about. All she wanted to do at this minute was get her clothes on.

'I'm fine,' she said quickly. 'In fact, if you'll just let me get up ...' Chad rose up on one elbow and stared down at her. She could see his face in the fire's glow. His eyes narrowed, the irises almost glowing with a golden light like the eyes of some great predatory animal. An apprehensive shudder ran through her. 'Why are you looking at me like that?' she asked.

'You damned near died on me, Jessica Howard,' he said gruffly, and then he shook his head and his expression softened. 'What the hell were you doing out there, Jessie?'

Images flashed into her mind and she drew a deep breath. 'I—I was looking for you,' she said slowly. 'I—I remember the branch breaking and the fire going out ...' She closed her eyes. 'I couldn't re-light it. The matches were soaked ... Yes, that's right. They were soaked and it was freezing in the cabin. So I decided to walk to the creek ...'

'To the creek,' he repeated, and she nodded her head. 'You were nowhere near the creek when I found you.'

'I followed your footsteps as long as I could,' she said slowly, opening her eyes and staring up at him. 'I remembered what you said about knowing where you were and all the rest and I tried, I tried, but it all got mixed up ...'

'You must have been wandering around out there for a couple of hours. You were like ice when I finally found you.' He shifted beneath the blankets and the length of his body brushed against hers. 'What is it?' he demanded as a tremor ran through her. 'Are you still cold?'

'No,' she said quickly, 'no, I'm fine now. But . . . what happened to me?' Her glance dropped to the tangle of blankets that covered them and she blushed. 'I—I only remember bits and pieces . . .'

'Hypothermia's what happened to you, Jessie. It never occurred to me to warn you about it. I mean, I figured you'd never be out of the cabin without me.'

'Hypothermia?' she repeated. 'What's that?'

'A killer,' he said shortly. 'It's what happens if you get too cold or wet and your temperature drops too quickly. You lose the ability to make decisions and the worst of it is, you don't realise it's happening. And then, your motor centres start shutting down. You can't walk or talk and finally, your heart shuts down, too.' He ran his hand lightly along her cheek. 'Thank God I found you before that happened. You were cold as marble, Jessie.'

'I . . . I really am OK now, Chad. I'd like to get up and . . . and get dressed . . .'

He smiled, his teeth flashing whitely in the shadows. 'Yeah, I wondered when we'd get around to that. In fact, I'd have thought that would be your first question.'

'Well,' she said quickly, 'of course. I mean, it is. It was. I wondered . . . I wondered . . .' She felt a rush of crimson flooding her cheeks. 'Can't we talk later, after I get . . .'

He grinned. 'Dressed? Sure, Jess. Just answer a question, OK? Do you remember getting undressed?'

'No—I mean, it's all fuzzy . . .' She took a deep breath, trying to maintain some semblance of dignity. 'I thought at first . . . The thing is, I thought I'd remember, and . . .'

Chad laughed softly. 'You're damned right you'd remember,' he said. 'I guarantee it.'

The colour in her cheeks deepened. 'Are you going to tease me or tell me what happened?'

'I told you what happened. You collapsed in the snow. I found you and brought you here.'

'And undressed me?' she asked in a small, unsteady voice.

He nodded his head. 'And put you to bed.'

Jessica cleared her throat. 'Where does it say that in the Boy Scout Manual?'

He grinned and touched his finger to the tip of her nose. 'I haven't got any idea.'

'But . . .'

'Any survival guidebook will tell you that the approved method of treatment for advanced hypothermia is to get the wet clothing off the victim . . .'

'Which you certainly did. But only one of us was the victim . . .'

'. . . get the wet clothing off the victim and then get the victim into a tub of warm water or under an electric blanket. In case you hadn't noticed, we haven't got either. In which case, you use body to body heat until the victim shows improvement.' He smiled crookedly. 'That means skin to skin, Jessie.'

'I see.' She ran her tongue over her lips and then she shifted carefully under the blanket, trying to move her body away from his. 'Well, I'm very grateful.'

'You're welcome,' he said solemnly.

'And now, since the victim shows improvement, I . . . I think she can get up.'

His eyes burned into hers. 'Is that what she wants?' he whispered.

A wildness raced through her. No, she thought, it's not what she wants. But she nodded. 'Yes,' she murmured. 'Turn your back, please.'

For the whisper of a heartbeat, she thought he was going to refuse. The possibility sent her pulse racing.

But finally he shrugged his shoulders and rolled away from her.

'You stay there,' he said. 'I'll get up.'

She turned her head away as he eased out from under the tangled blanket remnants, although not before she had a sudden glimpse of broad shoulders and muscled arms, painted golden bronze by the fire. The parts of her body that had been in contact with his through the long, cold night felt suddenly vulnerable, and she fought against the desire to reach out and pull him back down beside her. The hiss of cloth and zipper told her that he was putting his jeans on.

'I don't mean to seem ungrateful,' she said carefully.

He turned so quickly that she flinched. 'I don't want your gratitude, damn it,' he said angrily. 'I told you that before.'

'That isn't what I meant, Chad. But you did save my life ...'

'Forget it, OK?'

'Please, don't be angry. I couldn't stand it if you were.'

'I'm not angry.'

'Yes, you are,' she whispered. 'I can hear it in your voice and I don't ... I don't ...' Suddenly, a sob wrenched her body. Tears flooded down her cheeks and she covered her face with her hands.

'Jessie? Jessie, please, I'm sorry ...' He dropped to his knees beside her and caught her hands in his. 'Don't cry, Jessie,' he pleaded. 'I'm not angry at you.'

But the tears would not stop, no matter how she tried. 'I don't know what's the matter with me,' she sobbed. 'I feel awful.'

'It's the hypothermia,' he said. 'It makes you feel depressed.'

'We're going to die out here, aren't we? Tell me the truth, Chad.'

His hands slid beneath her and he lifted her, cradling her in his arms. 'Don't even think that,' he said in a fierce whisper. 'Of course we're not going to die. Haven't we been fine so far?' He shook her gently. 'Haven't we?'

She nodded her head and sniffed loudly. 'I guess.'

'You guess? Is that your idea of a vote of confidence? Here,' he said as she sniffed again, 'wipe your nose.' He held a piece of fabric to her nose—his shirt, she saw with fleeting surprise—and she did as he'd demanded. She sighed as he drew her head to his chest. 'That's better,' he said softly. 'Now, how about showing a little faith, Miss Howard? Haven't I taken pretty good care of us?'

'I didn't mean you hadn't.'

'I can't believe you'd doubt me, Jess.'

'Chad, I don't. I ...'

'I said I didn't want your gratitude, but I certainly expect your confidence.'

She shook her head in quick embarrassment. 'I know you've done a lot ...'

'Damned right I have. I crashed our plane, insulted your job and your city ...'

'What?' She looked at him in surprise. 'No, Chad, you ...'

'Marched you up a mountain and down a mountain, and then found you this absolutely palatial home in the finest little community this side of Manhattan Island ...'

A smile trembled on her mouth. 'Joke all you like, cowboy. You're the only reason we're alive. I know how much you've done.'

'I had to undress you, Jess. It was the only way.'

The sudden change in conversation caught her by

surprise. Her eyes met his and she nodded.

'Yes, I understand,' she said. 'Really.'

'It's just that it didn't happen quite the way I'd have liked.'

The softly spoken words stunned her. A piece of green wood spat and sizzled in the fireplace; the sound seemed to fill the cabin. She wanted to say something, anything, to fill the warp in time into which the cabin had suddenly drifted, but no words would come.

His arms tightened around her. 'I've made love to you in a thousand dreams, Jessie,' he whispered.

She closed her eyes and a tremor ran through her. 'Don't,' she begged.

He tilted her face up to his. 'Why not? Is it so terrible to think of me making love to you?'

She shook her head. 'No. God, no. But ...'

'Don't you know how I feel, Jessie?' His voice dropped to a silken whisper. 'Or is it that you don't want to know?'

That's it, she wanted to say, I don't want to know. But she couldn't lie to him or to herself, not now, not in the still, small hours of the night; not while the wind moaned outside the tiny cabin, not when the glow of Chad's eyes warmed her more than the flames in the fireplace. Hesitantly, she reached out and touched his cheek.

'Chad,' she said, searching for the words that would explain the insanity of all this, and then he turned his face into her palm and his lips burned against her flesh. It was the simplest of actions, but once it had happened, once she had felt that searing kiss, she knew she was lost. 'Chad,' she said again, but this time the single word was a surrender.

A sweet triumph surged through him at the sound of her voice. 'Dream with me, Jessie,' he whispered fiercely, as her hand touched his mouth again and then moved to the nape of his neck. 'Feel the way it was when I kissed you.' He drew aside the silken tangle of curls at her ear, and his lips brushed her skin. 'Your cheek,' he said, 'and your sweet mouth and your throat . . .' His head dropped towards hers; she sighed as his lips touched the soft curve of neck and shoulder.

His dream was hers. She knew it, had known it, almost from the first. He was touching her, whispering to her, and it was new and exciting, yet it was everything they had done and said to each other in a million other lifetimes. Jessica sighed and lifted her mouth to his.

'Tell me,' she whispered, 'tell me . . .'

'I lifted you into my arms and carried you to the fire.' His hands slid down her back, searing her flesh with their heat. 'I told you I wanted us to be able to see each other in the light of the flames, feel the heat of the fire on our bodies . . .' He drew her against him; she gasped as their bodies touched through the thin blanket. 'And you said . . .' His voice was low and thick with desire. 'You said you wanted me to make love to you, Jessie. You said you'd been waiting . . .'

It was too late to run away this time. She had gone too far, admitted too much. She could only sigh and touch him again, and admit the truth to herself as well as to him.

'Yes,' she whispered, 'I have been. I've been waiting all my life, for you, Chad . . .'

She moaned softly as his mouth sought hers. His kiss was sweet, his mouth cool. The faint rasp of his shadowy beard felt like a thousand tiny caresses against her skin. Her lips parted beneath his; when finally he drew away from her, she was breathless.

'I've kissed you until tasting your mouth wasn't enough,' he murmured. His hand slid across her back and she caught her breath as his fingers splayed along her ribs. 'That was when I undressed you, Jessie. I stripped away everything that separated us, all the layers, darling, all the superficial barriers, until there was nothing between us and we were only a man and a woman falling in love, and my hands and my mouth took the whole night to learn every part of you.'

She wound her arms tightly around his neck. In some dim, still-functioning corner of her mind, she realised she had known all along it would come to this. He was like no one she'd every imagined, yet he was the man for whom she'd been waiting. There would never be anyone else, and no one who had come before mattered now. It would all work out; it had to. Love had nothing to do with time or place or reality. Besides, for all she knew, life might end in this isolated piece of wilderness where they'd found shelter.

She sighed as his hand slid over the blanket between them, following the outline of her body. He murmured her name again, and then the blanket rustled and dropped to her waist. The heat of the fire was warm on her skin, but Chad's hands were warmer still. She closed her eyes as he touched her breasts, marvelling at how such a gentle caress could set her senses ablaze.

'You're so beautiful, Jessie,' he whispered. 'I tried not to think that before, when I undressed you . . .' He bent his head; she caught her breath as his lips found her breast. 'Do you want me? Tell me you want me, darling, tell me . . .'

'Yes,' she whispered with abandon, 'yes. Please make love to me, Chad. Please, my love . . .'

She lay back against the blankets, sliding her hands up his chest, tangling her fingers in the dark mat of hair, marvelling at the rapid thud of his heartbeat under her fingers. His skin was like fire-warmed silk; the muscles seeming to come alive beneath her touch. She lost herself in the soft sounds of pleasure he made as she touched him, and then, with a fierceness that surprised them both, she pulled his head down to hers.

Her face was a pale oval in the firelight's glow; her eyes were dark with passion, a reflection, he was certain, of his own.

'I love you,' he whispered. 'Jessie . . .'

'Yes,' she sighed, 'yes, oh yes, Chad. I love you.'

She watched his face through narrowed eyes. God, how beautiful he was, she thought. And there was a smell about him—that same scent of the outdoors she'd noticed before but now there was something more, something musky and male. He had invaded all her senses. It was as if he had become the world, the sun, the moon, the firmament in which the stars blazed forever . . .

'Is this what you want?' he murmured, touching her, kissing her, exciting her beyond rational thought. 'Tell me, Jessie. Tell me you love me.'

'Yes,' she gasped, 'Yes, yes . . .'

She wanted to tell him she would love him for ever, that even if the real world reclaimed them, she would be his. But his hands were touching her everywhere, learning secrets not even she had known, and it was too late to talk. It was too late to think. All Jessica could do was feel and wonder and love.

CHAPTER TEN

JESSICA ran her fingers through her tousled hair. The ends curled lightly around her fingers, clean and smooth from being washed yesterday morning with a tiny sliver of soap she'd dredged out of the bottom of Chad's backpack. She tucked her hair behind her ears and then brought it forward again. It needed cutting, she thought idly, wondering how it looked at this length. It was strange, not knowing what you looked like after ten days. Maybe it was better not to know when you had no make-up and only an exceedingly odd assortment of clothing to wear.

She buttoned her blouse and then slipped a sweater over her head. Chad said she looked beautiful but then, he might be just a bit prejudiced. He liked her hair this way, he had said, and she'd laughed and said she liked his beard. Some time during the long, dark night, she'd been awakened by the gentle rasp of his face against hers. The feeling had made her shiver with pleasure; Chad had felt her tremble in his arms and he'd whispered her name and shifted lower in their cocoon of blankets ...

They had been lovers for five nights—and five days, she thought, recalling the long, lazy hours they'd spent before the fireplace while a light snow fell outside. Lying in his arms, loving him with words as well as with her body, had brought their relationship a level of intimacy she'd never dreamed possible. She knew more about him than she had ever known about anyone. When she kissed his beard-roughened face, she was not just kissing Chad O'Bryan, the man—she was also kissing the little boy who had cried for days when his pony broke its leg in a chuckhole. And he knew things about her no one else knew. Little things, like how she'd despaired on her tenth birthday when she came down with the chicken pox and how her mother had gone ahead with her party anyway, holding it in the back yard, just outside her bedroom window, and how good she'd felt when she saw all the kids just outside the glass.

The long days and nights seemed to encourage an exchange of half-forgotten anecdotes and honest feelings. There was no need for the kind of superficial chitchat that often passed for conversation back in the city. She had never been very good at that kind of thing anyway; sometimes, standing around at one of the agency's parties, she played a little game with herself, trying to decide if the next man who approached her would talk first about the newest political scandal or the latest foreign film. Not that she and Chad only talked about serious issues—she smiled as she remembered . . .

Chad had been down at the creek, checking the fishing lines. She'd stayed behind to brew up a pot of after dinner bark and berry tea and then she'd grabbed her sweater and stepped out into the gathering darkness. The sun was setting over the mountains, turning them to purple and lilac, and a tightness had settled in her throat as she watched, wishing he were beside her, knowing that to see this alone was to experience only half the beauty of the moment. When he returned half an hour later, she was waiting for him in the cabin and the sky was dark.

'Chad,' she'd said, 'I wish you'd been here . . .'

And he had smiled and put his arms around her. 'The sunset,' he'd said. 'Yes, I know. I stopped and watched it, too. Somehow, I knew we were seeing it together.'

It was hard to realise they'd been strangers only ten

days ago, she thought with a sigh. In some ways, they were so alike that they could communicate without words. And yet, there were things about them that were so different, things that were a harsh reminder of the separate worlds from which they came. They'd had their first quarrel over the deer.

The animals had appeared in the meadow at the far end of Main Street two days ago, dark brown smudges against the white of the snow.

'Chad, look,' she'd said, 'there are deer in the meadow. Aren't they beautiful?'

'Yes, they are.' They'd watched the graceful animals for a few minutes and then he sighed. 'Give me my jacket, will you? And that sweater ... Thanks.'

She'd watched while he pulled on his outer clothing, sensing some dark undertone in his voice. 'Where are you going?' she asked at last. 'I thought you said you weren't going to check on the fish lines until later.'

'I'm not going to the creek, Jess. I want to get a closer look at the track those deer use.' She'd looked at him questioningly and finally he took her hands in his. 'Winter's coming on more quickly than I'd expected,' he said softly. 'And that means we're going to need meat soon.'

'But we have meat. The fish, I mean. You said there are plenty of them in the creek ...'

He shook his head. 'The creek's going to freeze over completely before long. That's going to make it harder to catch anything. Besides, fish don't provide enough fat.' He drew her to him and slipped his arms around her. 'Winters are pretty grim here, Jess. We'd never make it eating nothing but trout.'

He was right. She knew he was and she knew her reaction to the thought of killing the deer was illogical. Still, her eyes skidded past him to the window and to the animals in the meadow.

'I understand,' she said slowly. 'But those poor deer . . .'

'You don't understand,' he said roughly. 'I'm not going to let us die.'

Her eyes met his. 'I don't want to die. But . . .'

'Then start being a realist.'

She looked at him in silence and then, finally, she nodded.

'I really do understand,' she said. 'It's just hard for me—I haven't got the same background you do, Chad. I . . .'

'No,' he said sharply, 'I guess you haven't. The deer upset you, but that commercial your agency was supposed to film at Eagle Lake didn't.'

She had drawn back, startled by the roughness in his voice. 'What are you talking about? That was a commercial for coats . . . Her words trailed off like smoke. 'Fur coats,' she said softly. 'I—I guess I never thought of it that way before.'

'If you take an animal as part of the food chain, you're only doing what every other creature on this planet does to survive. And we are going to survive,' he'd said. 'I promised I'd get us out of here, and I will. I swear it.'

Jessica sighed and added some wood to the fire. She was convinced Chad would, indeed, get them out of the mountains. He was the most determined man she'd ever known. And yet, and yet . . . She bent down and stirred the fire with a stick until the flames sprang up again. She had almost told him she had no desire to leave Coleman's Creek. Of course, she hadn't said it—it was a crazy thought. She had a life and a career to go back to. So did he, for that matter. He'd talked about how much he wanted his grant to come through. If it did, he'd be able to go back to Alaska for another six months and study his wolf pack, and she'd probably never see him again. Unless he asked her to go with him, she thought suddenly. Unless ...

'That's crazy, Jessica Howard,' she murmured aloud. 'Crazy ...'

The door swung open and cold air swirled into the cabin. Chad came into the room laughing, stamping snow from his feet. 'A little strange, OK. But never crazy, Jessie.'

She smiled as she crossed the room towards him. 'I was just telling myself you'd get here eventually and that I wouldn't have to eat the empty skillet for breakfast.'

'Breakfast wasn't terribly co-operative this morning,' he said with a quick grin. 'It took a while to come up with bacon and eggs for two, but here it is, all cleaned and ready to cook.'

'Good,' she said, carefully taking the fish from him with two fingers. 'That's just the way I buy them at the A&P.'

'Is the tea ready? I'm freezing.'

'It's ready, master,' Jessica said, laying the trout in the skillet and shoving it into the hot coals at the rear of the hearth. 'I wouldn't want you to freeze to death.'

His arms slipped around her waist and she leaned back against him. 'I know,' he chuckled. 'I'm glad I taught you the treatment for hypothermia.'

Jessica smiled as he nibbled her neck. 'You're insufferable,' she said.

'I'm just trying to teach you everything I know about survival,' he said. 'And I've been told that I'm a pretty fair teacher.'

'Where's your modesty?' she teased.

Chad grinned and turned her in his arms. 'I meant a real teacher, Jessie.'

'Sure,' she said, smiling up at him. 'What did you

teach? ABCs to wolves?'

'Biology, Miss Howard. To freshmen and sopho-
mores at Hunter College.'

'Hunter College?' she asked slowly. 'In Manhattan?'
He nodded and she tilted her head to one side. 'Really?'

'Sure. Didn't I tell you I'd done some teaching
between grants? Hunter was one of the places that liked
me a lot. Told me they'd take me back if ever I decided I
wanted to make a career out of teaching.' He grinned at
her. 'Surprised?'

'Surprised?' Jessica shook her head. Surprised wasn't
the right word, she thought. Delighted was more like it.
Thrilled, maybe or ecstatic ... Her cowboy didn't have
to ride off into the Alaskan sunset after all. 'Are you
telling me you can get a job teaching right in New York?
Why, that's wonderful.'

'It would be if I wanted it. I'll probably take it if my
grant doesn't come through but, God, I hate the
thought. Stuffy leacture halls, crowded classrooms,
schedules to meet ...'

'But it's a good school, isn't it? I mean ...'

'Sure, it's a terrific school. But I don't like the idea of
spending my life in a classroom. Besides, I have a better
idea. If I get my grant ...'

'Your grant,' she said slowly. 'You mean, you'd
rather go to Alaska.'

'Of course.'

She felt an unreasoning anger flush her cheeks. 'Well,
then, I hope it comes through,' she said stiffly, moving
out of his arms. 'Let me see if our breakfast is ready.'

Chad reached towards her. 'Hey,' he said, 'what did I
do?'

'Give me that rag, will you? This skillet's hot as
blazes.'

'Jessie ...'

'It's more than ready. As a matter of fact, it's charred. Sit down,' she said, setting the skillet on the table. 'I'll get the tea.'

Chad glanced at her as she moved across the floor. 'Jessie, listen, don't be angry.'

'Angry? Why should I be angry?'

'I told you I prefer field work. The guys in the classrooms are doing an important job, but they can only teach what somebody else discovers.' He pulled the stool closer to the table and sat down. 'I didn't become a wildlife biologist because I like test tubes and chalk, Jess. Don't you understand?'

Jessica sat opposite him and stared at the charred trout. Yes, she understood. What had got into her, anyway? Chad was a maverick; she'd known that from the start. He wasn't about to give up a life he loved for her. If he did, the cowboy she'd fallen in love with would disappear under layers of tweedy academia.

Suddenly, it all seemed so simple. She'd had the same crazy thought before, but she'd shoved it aside. But what was so crazy about it? His career was established; hers hadn't really begun yet. It was a lot easier for her to walk away from New York than it would be for him to walk away from his work. Besides, where she spent her life wasn't half as important as who she spent it with. All she needed was Chad. Her fork clattered to the table and she took a deep breath.

'Chad, listen. I've been thinking about Alaska . . .'

'It's more than Alaska,' he said suddenly. She looked up at him as if he'd just said something in Greek. 'There are lots of places to study, Jess. And other animals besides wolves. I've always wanted to do some work on wild dogs, for instance. Jackals . . .'

'Jackals,' she said tonelessly.

'Yeah. I spent my senior year on internship in Africa

with Ian Douglas. He was doing a study of lions ...'

Jessica shoved her chair back from the table and got to her feet. 'Africa,' she repeated evenly. 'Not Alaska.'

A bewildered expression settled on Chad's face. 'No, of course not. Anyway, I did some preliminary work on jackals. In fact, when Douglas asked me to go to Brazil ...'

He jumped as she slammed the canteen on the table. 'Sorry,' she said stiffly. 'It must have slipped. Let me get this straight, Chad. You went to Brazil and Africa ...'

'Well, I hadn't decided the area I wanted to investigate for my Master's thesis, so I went along with him. He was doing a study on jaguars. And then I decided to do my work on wolves ...'

'And that's when you went to Alaska.'

He shook his head. 'Actually, I went to Isle St Royale that time.' Chad hitched the stool closer to the table and his eyes sought hers. 'Do you understand what I'm saying, Jess? Damn it, stop looking at me that way!'

'What way?' she asked, amazed at the calmness of her voice.

'The way you looked at me on the plane,' he said roughly. 'As if I were some other form of life ... Jessie, I'm trying my damnedest to tell you something. I knew it wouldn't be easy, but you're making it hard as hell.'

There was something in his voice, a twisted, rough edge ... Jessica looked at him and the expression in his eyes made her heart turn over. Of course, he was trying to tell her something! Did he think she was dense? Reality lay beyond Coleman's Creek—that's what he was telling her. Dream with me, he'd said, and she had. But dreams weren't real, not even if you wanted them to be with all your heart and soul ... But their dream hadn't ended yet, she thought. And she would hang on to it as long as the world let her.

'I know what you're trying to tell me,' she murmured. 'You don't have to spell it out.'

'But we've got to talk about what happens after we get out of here, Jessie. I want you to understand ...'

She shook her head and laid her fingers lightly across his mouth. 'I do,' she said quickly. 'I know we have no future, Chad. I could no more live in your world than you could live in mine.'

He caught her hand in both of his. 'Do you mean that?' he demanded.

'Yes,' she whispered. 'Yes, I ...' Her softly spoken words were drowned out by a roaring noise that made the walls tremble. Jessica's eyes widened with fright. 'Chad? What was that?'

He stared at her and then he took a deep breath. 'It's a helicopter,' he said tonelessly. 'They've found us, Jessie.'

This was the moment, then, she thought. But where was the jubilation? Where was the sense of relief? Why was she suddenly blinking back tears? She nodded and pushed back her chair.

'I guess we'd better open the door,' she said finally.

Chad's hands tightened on hers. 'Jessie,' he said thickly, 'Jessie ...'

There was a tightness in her throat. His face was a reflection of what she was feeling; there was a sorrow in his eyes, an emptiness in their topaz depths. She wanted to tell him she understood, that it had been a wonderful dream and it was no one's fault it was over, but she was afraid to speak. All she could do was force a smile to her lips. She pulled her hand free of his and turned away so that he would not see the tears spilling down her cheeks.

'Damn it,' Chad said, 'Damn it ...'

She turned again as she heard his footsteps, watching as he strode to the door and flung it open. Slowly, she picked up her sweater and pulled it on, following him silently out into Main Street.

A helicopter sat in the snowy meadow at the end of the street, its whirling blades churning up a miniature blizzard. Chad moved out into the street with Jessica following close behind. They watched in silence as a man scrambled to the ground and ran towards them.

'You've got to be Chad O'Bryan and Jessica Howard. We'd just about given up hope. Hey, you two,' he added with a laugh, 'smile! Don't you understand? It's over.'

Jessica shuddered. Their rescuer's words were more chilling than the wind whipping down Main Street.

Yes, she thought, it certainly was.

CHAPTER ELEVEN

FORTY storeys above Manhattan's streets, the sounds of traffic are barely audible. The snarling cars and trucks below, the hurrying pedestrians, all seem to be performers in some great pantomime. On a day in October, a day of bright leaves and warm sun, Jessica Howard pressed her forehead against her office window and stared down at the street. Plane trees still festooned with clutches of golden autumn leaves fought bravely against the grey efficiency of the city. Jessica sighed and laid her palms against the cool glass. It would be so nice to be able to open the window, she thought wistfully, so nice to smell the trees and the Indian summer air instead of the machine cooled and filtered stuff pumping through ventilating louvers in the ceiling. It was ridiculous to seal windows this way. Chad would have said ...

She turned away abruptly and walked across her tiny office. Ten o'clock, she thought, glancing at her wrist, and she hadn't done a thing about the report on her desk even though she had a meeting with a client in less than two hours. Besides, even if the window could be opened, there wouldn't be much to smell besides automobile exhaust fumes. That was one of the things Chad had said about New York ...

Damn! She stopped in mid-stride and frowned. What had she done with the survey results that went with the report? Buried them in the filing cabinet, most probably, because there wasn't a drawer or a cubby-hole in the desk, or what Allen Associates insisted on calling a desk. Actually, it was a glass and chrome table. Chad would have laughed at the idea of passing off something with no drawers as a desk, just as he'd have laughed at calling this oversized cupboard a office . . .

'For goodness' sake,' Jessica said loudly, slamming the top drawer of the filing cabinet closed. What on earth was the matter with her? Chad O'Bryan was a two-week-old memory, yet his shadow seemed to be lurking everywhere today. Maybe it had been a mistake to cut through Central Park on her way to work this morning. It had seemed like a fine idea on such a marvellous day, but the trees and the grass and the sun sparkling on the boat lake had all conspired to make her think of him—not that there was anything unique about that, she thought unhappily. She thought about him in the empty silence of her apartment, and in the dark house of the night and . . .

Jessica tossed the file down on her desk and slid into her chair. But she didn't think about him here. That was the only good thing about her promotion—her 'welcome-home present', her boss had called it. She disliked her new job, but there was so much to learn and to do that it kept her mindlessly occupied from morning until night. And that was precisely what she'd needed, from her very first day back at work.

'I'm taking you to lunch, Jessica,' Jack Allen had announced, snatching her away from all the office well-wishers. 'We have things to talk about.'

Was he going to fire her? she'd wondered, grabbing her jacket. Everybody had told her the girl who'd replaced her for the past two weeks hadn't done her job well, but you could never tell.

'Is there a problem, Mr Allen?'

'Call me Jack,' he said, hurrying her along Third Avenue. 'This great little Mexican place opened while you were gone, Jessica. Everybody goes there—wait until you see how authentic it is.'

He wasn't going to fire her, she thought, breathing a sigh of relief. Not over tostadas and guacamole, anyway.

'Great. I love Mexican food.'

They settled in at a wood-patterned plastic table and gave their orders to a waitress with a Brooklyn accent. Jack Allen pushed aside the bottle of ketchup that adorned the centre of the table and smiled at her. So much for authenticity, she thought, returning his smile. Chad would have got a kick out of this place ...

'So, Jessica, how are you feeling? You look a little, I don't know, pale or something.'

'No,' she said brightly, 'I'm fine. I guess I lost a little weight, that's all.'

Her boss lit a cigarette and she coughed discreetly as a cloud of smoke drifted towards her. 'You stopped smoking, huh? Well, at least there was some benefit to being stuck out in the tail-end of nowhere for two weeks.' He smiled and leaned back in the rattan and brass chair. 'I've got a welcome home present for you, dear.'

'Well, that's nice,' she said slowly, hoping it would be a raise in salary and not a left-over bottle of cologne from Allen Associates' Christmas gifts to junior female employees. 'Thank you.'

'My phone's been ringing all morning, Jessica. Clients keep calling and asking about you. You're quite a celebrity.'

Jessica smiled uncomfortably. 'By next week, nobody will remember my name.'

'You let me worry about that,' Allen said, folding his hands on his paunch. 'You know, people love to deal with celebrities.' A broad smile lit his face. 'So I've decided to make you an assistant account executive.'

She stared at him in astonishment. 'A what?'

'Surprised, right? I know you don't have any experience with clients, but you're a bright girl. You can work with Paul or Sheryl or whoever needs you, and once you learn the ropes . . .'

'Mr Allen, it's not that I'm ungrateful, but . . . Look, I don't know the first thing about that end of advertising.'

'Nobody does, when they start out. You'll learn, Jessica.'

'Yes, but, you see, I really want to—the thing is, I've been studying photography for a couple of years and—well—as a matter of fact, I took some pictures in those mountains that look pretty good . . .'

Her boss took a last puff on his cigarette and then ground it into the plastic soil of an artificial cactus on the floor beside them.

'A celebrity to take pictures? What kind of mileage could we get from that? Besides, I already have a photographer.'

'But . . .'

'Listen, if it makes you happy, go show your pictures to him. Tell Hans I said to take a look and see if we can use one or two for background.' He smiled winningly. 'And while you wait to become the world's next Richard Avedon, we'll move you into your own office and raise your salary seventy-five bucks a week. How's that sound?'

It had sounded like something her bank account couldn't afford to pass up, and so she'd moved into this oversized cupboard and dropped her pictures off at Hans' studio the same day.

'Mr Allen said . . .'

'Right. He told me. I'll take a look.'

'I . . . I think some of them might be . . .'

'I'll let you know,' he'd said firmly, and that had been the last she'd heard from the man.

Jessica opened the file and glanced unseeingly at the survey results she needed for the upcoming meeting. Well, what had she expected Hans to say, after all? Her photos were good, not terrific. It was just that the raw beauty of the mountains had come through in almost every shot, even though she hadn't used special lenses or filters. There were a couple of pictures of Chad on the trail and beside the fire that were exceptional. She'd somehow managed to capture his strength and honesty and . . .

God, she felt restless. If only she could slip away for an hour or so. The Zoo would be beautiful today. It was too late for summer crowds, and too early for groups of school children to be traipsing through the wooded land; she'd have the place all to herself. Autumn was the best time to go there, although she liked it on snowy winter days, too. She sighed and glanced at the window. It was impossible to think that winter had already arrived in Coleman's Creek but the little cabin on Main Street was probably window deep in snow by now. If she closed her eyes, she could still see the flames dancing in the fireplace and remember how they warmed the room and kept the cold at bay, not that she'd needed any warmth other than Chad's arms and mouth . . .

'Stop it,' she whispered, closing her eyes and putting her hands to her head. If she let the memory of him into her office, she was lost. It was over: why couldn't she accept that? She'd gone on to a new job and he—for all she knew, he was in Alaska. After all, their return to civilisation had made instant celebrities of them both. Maybe he'd got the grant he'd wanted so badly. Maybe . . .

What did it matter? Their love affair had ended that last day in Coleman's Creek. Boarding the helicopter for the trip to Cheyenne had just sealed what their talk in the cabin had started. It seemed so simple, she thought, leaning back wearily and resting her head against the chair. But that was before she'd realised that the end of their love affair had nothing to do with the end of love.

They'd made the flight to Cheyenne in silence. You couldn't talk over the noise of the engine and the whirling rotors, which was just as well, because they'd said all there was to say in the cabin. She remembered staring blindly out the window, for once in her life unafraid and damned near unaware of the fact that she was flying, praying that the euphoria of their rescue would replace the pain within her.

Two deputy sheriffs had been waiting for them in Cheyenne. Separate cars whisked them to a hospital where doctors poked and prodded until everybody was satisfied that they were in good health. Jessica had phoned her parents in Ohio, assuring them that she was fine, which they found slightly bewildering because they had only just returned from vacation and had no idea she wasn't. By the time she saw Chad in the hospital corridor again, word of their rescue had got out and they were surrounded by local television and newspaper reporters. And there was somebody there from Wind River Charters who insisted Chad had to go with him to the airport and file reports with the company and with the Federal Aeronautics Administration.

'Jessie . . .' he'd said. 'Jessie, we'll talk when I get back.'

She'd smiled and nodded her head. 'Sure,' she'd said, knowing it was a lie, knowing they had nothing left to say. Salvation lay in getting back to her job, her city, her apartment—the sooner she got back to her world, the sooner she'd get rid of the heaviness that had settled just under her heart. As soon as the door closed after him, she turned to one of the nurses.

'When is the next flight to New York?' she asked in an urgent tone. 'Could you find out for me, please?'

'Sure, but . . . Don't you think you should rest here for a day or two, Miss Howard?'

'Just find out and get me a seat on it, please,' Jessica said firmly.

As luck would have it, she'd had to wait four long hours for the next flight. At first, she flinched each time she heard footsteps, certain it was Chad, hoping it wouldn't be and wishing it would, but he didn't return. Not that she was surprised. It must have occurred to him, too, that a clean break was best. And that had been the last she'd heard from him, not that any of the office gossips believed it.

Planning a reunion with that guy, Jessica?' the receptionist had teased. 'After all, you must have got to know each other pretty well, huh?'

The questions grew more specific after two of the local tabloids picked up pictures of her and Chad from the Cheyenne papers. 'What did you and that man do for two weeks, Miss Howard?' one of her women clients had asked just yesterday. 'You never told me the guy was so good-looking!'

I never told you anything, Jessica had thought sadly. I never told you how funny he was or how strong or how much I miss the sound of his voice or the touch of his hands . . .

'Hello? Jessica, are you there?'

Somebody was hammering on the closed door to her office. Quickly, Jessica rubbed her hands across her eyes. 'Yes,' she called, 'come in, please.'

The door swung open and Hans peered into the room. 'My God, it's barely big enough for a midget,' he said glumly. 'Is there room for both of us?'

'Only if we don't both inhale at the same time,' she

said. 'How are you, Hans? This is an unexpected pleasure.' She waved her hand at the low-slung chrome and leather chair facing her desk. 'It's more comfortable than it looks,' she said with a quick smile.

The photographer eased his gangly form into the chair and shifted nervously. 'I never liked these damned things,' he said. 'I'm always afraid they're going to attack and swallow me whole.' He looked around the room and shook his head. 'My supply cupboard is bigger than this, Jessica. Are you sure you got a promotion? Maybe the agency's doing a test on claustrophobia.'

Jessica laughed. 'You mean, you're not impressed by my palatial office? How have you been, Hans? Is my replacement working out?'

'Who knows? She's always leaving shoots a few minutes early so she can run across town and try to sell her sketches to somebody or other. Seems she's a frustrated dress designer. She's not like you were, Jessica. You kept your mind on business.'

'That's the first compliment you ever gave me,' Jessica answered with a quick grin. 'I can't believe it.'

'Don't let it go to your head,' Hans said dourly. 'All I meant was that you did what you got paid to do. You didn't spend all your time reminding me that you really wanted to do something else.'

She shrugged her shoulders and smiled. 'What for? I showed you my pictures once and you didn't think they were any good.'

'I told you the processing needed improvement,' he answered, pointing his finger at her. 'I never said your work wasn't good.'

'You never said it was, Hans.'

He sighed and crossed his legs. 'What'd you expect, Jessica? Applause? That's not me and you know it. Actually, your shots showed promise.'

'Promise,' she repeated, and he nodded. Well, she thought, so much for the photographs she'd given him of Coleman's Creek and the Wind River Wilderness. He was going to let her down easy.

'Thanks, Hans. I'm grateful to you for looking at my stuff. I'd appreciate it if you could drop the prints off some time. Or I can come by the studio and pick them up.'

'The ones you showed me last time showed promise, Jessica.' He leaned forward and tossed a piece of paper on her desk. 'The ones from the Windy Mountains . . .'

'Wind River Mountains,' she said automatically, picking up the paper. 'What's this?'

'The ones from Wind River are different. No more promise . . .'

She winced. 'Jesus, Hans . . .'

'They show talent,' he said, grinning at her. 'You did a damned good job with those shots, Jessica.'

'Well, thanks,' she said slowly, a soft blush of pleasure colouring her cheeks. 'I didn't really have much of a camera. The Corona AutoFocus is a nice little thing, but . . .'

The photographer nodded. 'Exactly. No filters, no exotic lenses—that's what I told my buddy over at Corona.'

'Hold it, Hans. What are you talking about? The Corona Camera Company, you mean?'

'I've got an old friend in their advertising department. He liked your pictures, Jessica. Call him—he'll tell you so himself.' He pointed a finger at the piece of crumpled paper in her hand. 'That's his name and number.'

'Thanks,' she said slowly, looking down at the scrawled name and number, 'but I don't understand . . .'

Hans smiled. 'Corona's been working up a big campaign built around the fact that this camera will

deliver quality prints in places other cameras won't.
Didn't you tell me you carried that little number with
you through a plane crash and up a mountain and God
only knows what else?' She nodded her head and he
smiled again. 'Hell, do you know what kind of publicity
that is?'

'You mean . . .' She swallowed hard. It was too much
to hope for. 'You mean they might want to buy some of
my pictures? Oh, Hans . . .'

'Jessica, you're not listening. They want to make you
and your photos the springboard for their whole
campaign. Who knows where it all ends? Maybe with
you and your Corona on the moon.' He grinned and
unwound his legs. 'Listen,' he said, getting to his feet,
'call this guy, OK?'

She shook her head and stared at him blankly. 'I don't
believe it.'

'The public already knows your name, Jessica. The
plane crash was one thing, but surviving it and coming
back to life two weeks later is another. Not everybody
does that, and not everybody shows up clutching rolls of
film taken on a brand new little camera.' Hans walked to
the door and tapped it lightly. 'Hear that?' he said with a
wink. 'It's opportunity knocking, kid. You'd better grab
it before it gets away.'

'I . . . I don't know how to thank you, Hans,' Jessica
stammered, rising to her feet. 'I don't know what to
say . . .'

A grudging smile lit the photographer's dour features.
'Look, kid, somebody gave me a helping hand years ago
when I got started. I'm just returning the favour. You
can do the same for somebody else some day.'

'They really want to buy my pictures?' she repeated.
'Corona?'

'You've got it, Jessica. By the way, do you have a

release from that guy?'

'Release?'

Hans nodded. 'You'll need a signed release from that pilot. You've got some terrific shots of him they're sure to want.' He smiled and opened the door. 'I guess you had other things on your mind when you were taking those pictures, huh? Well, you can get his signature easily enough.'

'I can't,' she said quickly. 'I don't even know where he is, and . . .'

'Trace him through the airline he worked for, Jessica. No problem, right?'

Jessica swallowed drily. 'Right,' she said evenly. 'No problem.'

CHAPTER TWELVE

JESSICA turned up the collar of her corduroy jacket and tucked her hands deep into her pockets. A cool wind, blowing unchecked through the skeletal trees, swept the hair back from her face. The last scarlet and gold leaves of autumn had turned the winding path into a carpet of colour that crunched under her booted feet. She looked up as a harsh cry reverberated through the late afternoon silence. There were always peacocks wandering free on the grounds of the Bronx Zoo; she'd photographed them often enough, but she never got used to their calls. It seemed a joke of nature that such beautiful creatures should have such raucous voices.

The Zoo was all but deserted. The only other people she'd seen had been an elderly couple at the Polar Bear enclosure, laughing as they watched a great white bear ride a concrete slide into a pool of water. It was the sort of raw, late October day that made New Yorkers remember the heat and humidity of the summer past with kindness, the sort of day Jessica loved because she knew she and her camera would have the Zoo to themselves. But there was no camera dangling from her neck today and no bulging equipment bag on her shoulder. She wasn't here to take pictures; she was here to meet Chad O'Bryan.

She pushed back her sleeve and glanced at her watch. Chad had said he'd be at the wolf enclosure at half past three and it was almost that now. He probably wouldn't wait if she were late, she thought, and her footsteps quickened. It had taken some fast talking to get him to agree to meet her at all. But she'd been determined,

especially after the trouble she'd had tracking him down.
Wind River Charters had given her a phone number in
Denver. She'd dialled it with trembling fingers only to
hear a flat, computer-generated voice tell her the
number had been disconnected. Hunter College had
been her next try; she'd started with the Biology
Department and then talked her way from one office to
the next without finding anyone who knew Chad's
current address or phone number.

'Look,' she'd said to the people at Corona Camera,
'there are lots of pictures without Mr O'Bryan in them.
Can't you just use those?'

'The shots of him have a certain quality, Miss
Howard. Surely you can see that.'

Yes, she could indeed. Chad looked as if he belonged
in those mountains and in that cabin. They were good
pictures and she was proud of them, although there were
others that were even better, others she would never
show anyone or sell at any price. She'd looked at them
again last night and then tucked them away, wishing she
had either the courage to throw them out or hang them
on the wall.

'Anyway, I doubt if he's going to sign a realease,'
she'd said finally. 'You don't know how stubborn he can
be.'

'You let us worry about that,' the Corona Camera
executives replied pleasantly. 'We think Dr O'Bryan will
be pleased to hear that we're interested in making a
considerable contribution to his work.'

Doctor O'Bryan ... She'd teased him about his title
often enough but, in the expensively decorated offices of
the Corona Camera Company, the title had a different
ring. But it helped put things in perspective. It wasn't
Chad she was seeking, it was a man who had a doctorate
in biology, a man with whom she had business to con-
duct. She located him, finally, in the most unexpected

way, seated in her dentist's waiting room, reading a current issue of International Geography magazine. There, buried in a column about recent award winners, was the name Chad O'Bryan, BS, MS, PhD, and the news that he'd just been awarded a grant to continue his studies of Alaskan wolf pack structure. Interesting, Jessica thought, closing the magazine. Chad had told her how difficult it was to get funding for his project. Apparently, becoming an instant celebrity hadn't hurt his career, either.

She'd phoned International Geography that same afternoon and wheedled a Manhattan phone number out of them, half expecting it to lead to another dead end. But she dialled it dutifully, and waited while it rang and rang and then, at the last second, the phone was answered and she heard Chad's voice for the first time in almost a month. He sounded snappish and irritable, as if the ring of the telephone had taken him from something important.

'Yes? What is it?'

Jessica swallowed drily. 'Hello, Chad,' she said hesitantly. 'It's Jessica. How have you been?'

'Busy,' he said after a lengthy silence. 'And you?'

'Fine, just fine.' She closed her eyes and tangled the telephone cord in her fingers. Why had she ever agreed to do this? Ten times all the Corona contracts in the world weren't worth it. She took a deep breath. 'I have some business to discuss with you.' The flat silence of the mute telephone added to her discomfort. 'I—I took some pictures, remember? And I've had an offer for them.'

'I'm glad to hear you made a sale,' he said politely. 'But I don't see how that involves me.'

'I'd like you to sign a release. You're in some of the photos, you see, and——'

'Forget it, Jessica. I'm not about to let you or anybody

else use a picture of me.'

'It's not "anybody", Chad, it's the Corona Camera Company. They want——'

'I don't care what they want.'

'They'll make a contribution to that field study you're going to do——'

'I don't want their money, Jessica. I've got legitimate financing.'

'Are you saying Corona's money isn't legitimate?'

'Look,' he said, 'they want to sell cameras, right? They're not interested in anything but dollars and cents.'

God, she thought, pacing as far as the telephone cord would permit, how self-righteous he sounded. The purist knew everything, as always. How on earth could she ever have forgotten that?

'Everybody's interested in dollars and cents,' she said. 'Even you, Chad. Your wolf study couldn't be done without money, could it?'

'That's different,' he said sharply. 'My study isn't commercial.'

'For heaven's sake, all Corona wants to do is sell cameras, not used cars.' She took a steadying breath. 'Look, they want to buy my pictures. Do you have any idea what that means to me? They want to make my photographs the centre of their advertising campaign.'

'You mean they want to use my mountains and my ghost town and my face.'

'Oh, don't be ridiculous. You don't own Coleman's Creek or the Wind River Range.'

'I sure as hell own this face,' he said smugly.

Jessica collapsed into a chair. 'If you'd just meet with them ...'

'No.'

'Chad, please ...'

'I'm busy, Jessica. I haven't got time to waste talking

to Madison Avenue phonies. I'm only going to be in town for another couple of days ...'

'They can see you whenever you like,' she interrupted. 'Tomorrow ...'

'I'll be at the Zoo tomorrow,' he said. 'I have to finish some observations I started a few months back.'

'But ...'

'Goodbye, Jessica.'

'Chad, wait ... Suppose I meet you there? I can show you the pictures Corona wants to use. You might change your mind when you see them.' The suggestion was out before she had time to think about it. She held her breath, wishing she could call it back. He'd made her angry and desperate, but she wasn't ready to face him, not yet, certainly not tomorrow, maybe never ...

The silence that greeted her suggestion was interminable. Finally, she heard the outrush of his breath.

'All right,' he said, his voice husky and harsh. 'Three-thirty. At the wolf enclosure.'

'Thank you,' she'd begun, and then she'd heard the metallic click of the line being disconnected.

There it was now, just ahead. The wolf enclosure. Her footsteps slowed as she approached the well wooded area. No one was there, which was no great surprise. The enclosure was meant to resemble a forest as much as possible and the pack was free to roam within it. You couldn't always see the wolves; you had to be patient and quiet, and most people were neither. She stopped and looked at her watch again. It was just past three-thirty— had Chad changed his mind? Perhaps he'd already been here and gone.

'Hello, Jessica.'

The sound of his voice touched her like a familiar caress. She turned slowly—yes, there he was, exactly the way she remembered, tall and lean and still dressed as if he were going out to herd cattle. Her heart started racing. God, how she'd missed him ...

'Hello, Chad.' She swallowed and then managed a forced smile. 'I wish I knew how you do that. I never heard you coming.'

'I've been waiting for you,' he said, walking slowly towards her. His eyes swept over her and he smiled. 'You look great.'

'So do you,' she said, returning his smile. 'I see you got rid of the beard but kept the moustache.'

He grinned and ran his finger along his upper lip. 'Yeah, I decided to give it a try. What do you think?'

'I like it,' she said honestly. It was true, she thought, she did. It gave his rugged face an urbane masculinity. Get to it, Jessica, she told herself sharply. You're here for a purpose.

'Thanks for meeting me,' she said. 'I brought the pictures.'

'I told you, I had some work here anyway. I got lucky with a grant and I'm leaving New York in a couple of days. I'm going back to Alaska.'

Jessica nodded her head. 'I read about it. You must be very pleased.'

He shrugged his shoulders. 'I'm looking forward to it.'

'I can imagine. It's great to do something innovative in your own field, isn't it?' She pulled a large envelope out of her shoulder-bag and held it out to him. 'That's how I feel about these pictures,' she added brightly. 'I think I caught something special in them. Won't you please take a look? I know you're afraid publishing them will be an invasion of your privacy, but ...'

'Of course it will,' he said, taking the envelope from her. 'But I know it means a lot to you, Jessica. I thought about it last night and ...' He opened the clasp and pulled out the photographs. 'There can't be too many of me, anyway. I don't recall you pointing the camera in my direction all that much.' His voice drifted away as he began to sift through the photos. 'Well,' he said after a while, 'I've got to admit you're good.' He looked up and smiled politely. 'You've captured the feeling of the mountains and the town.' He glanced down at the pictures again and fanned through the last few. 'I didn't know you'd taken so many of me. This one on the trail's pretty good ...'

He was going to sign the release. She was sure of it. Thank you, she thought, thank you ... Suddenly, the expression on his face changed. He stared at the last photograph and when he looked up again, his eyes were cold and flat.

'Forget it,' he said. 'I'm not signing anything.' She gasped as he crumpled the photo and let it tumble to the ground. 'That's what I think of your picture. And here's the rest of them.'

The envelope fell at her feet and she stared at him, stunned. 'Who do you think you are?' she whispered. 'That's my property ...' Her voice broke and she bent and picked up the picture. 'This photo belongs to me,' she said, opening the crumpled paper and smoothing it out. 'I took it and I own it. You have no right to destroy it.'

'It's better to destroy it cleanly than to sell it,' he growled.

'Don't be ridiculous,' she said. 'This picture ...' She looked down at the creased photograph in her hand and then back at Chad. 'This picture ...' The colour drained from her face and she glanced at the photograph again. It was a candid shot of Chad, one she had almost destroyed a dozen times because just looking at it made her remember things it was best to forget. He was squatting before the fire without his shirt ... She had taken the picture one snowy afternoon after long hours spent in his arms.

'I want to add some wood to the fire,' he'd murmured, and she had laughed softly.

'Why?' she'd whispered. 'Aren't you warm enough, darling? I certainly am.'

She looked up blindly. 'This isn't for sale,' she said. 'It shouldn't have been in the envelope.'

'Why not, Jessica? Didn't Corona offer enough?'

'Chad, please—you must believe me. I wouldn't . . . I couldn't . . . Not something like this . . .'

'Why not?' he asked coldly. 'After all, it's only a photograph of a guy you knew in another lifetime, isn't it?'

She shook her head from side to side. 'You know better than that, Chad. You know . . .'

'What? What do I know, Jessie?' He reached out and grasped her shoulders, his fingers biting through her corduroy jacket and into her flesh. 'The only thing I know is that I was a fool to meet you today.'

'Chad, please—I would never sell that photo . . .'

'Come on, Jessie. All it is is a souvenir of a time when you played house with a dumb cowboy.'

Tears shone in her eyes. 'You know it wasn't like that.'

'What I know is that only a dumb cowboy would have let himself believe we had something special.'

She shook her head. 'We did . . .'

'Don't lie to me, damn it. What we had was fine as long as the real world was far away. But you couldn't wait to get back to New York, once you had the chance.'

She shook her head. 'No,' she whispered, 'that's not true . . .'

'Or was it that you couldn't wait to get away from me, Jessie? Did I scare you that last day in the cabin, when I was falling all over myself trying to tell you that I knew a way we could be together for the rest of our lives?'

She brushed the tears from her eyes and stared at him in amazement. 'What are you talking about? All you talked about that day was how impossible it would be for you to make room in your life for me.'

'Are you crazy? I ...'

'Telling me how you couldn't wait to get back to Alaska and that you were already looking forward to studying hyenas in Africa ...'

'Jackals,' he said automatically.

'I don't care if it's jackals or hyenas or penguins,' she said furiously. 'All I know is that you made damned sure I understood that you weren't interested in staying around just because of me.'

'You're wrong, Jessie ...'

She pulled free of his grasp. 'And now,' she said, staring at him, 'now, you want to make it sound as if I walked away from you. What's the matter, Dr O'Bryan? Did you have an attack of morals? Does it hurt to remember how badly you treated me?'

'I don't know what in hell you're raving about, Jessica Howard. I thought I had this terrific idea that last day at Coleman's Creek ...'

'Oh, it was a marvellous idea,' she said bitterly, turning away from him. 'You were going to make sure I didn't forget that our ... our liaison was a temporary one ...'

Chad grasped her wrist. 'Don't you walk away from me,' he said angrily. 'I let you get away with that once but not any more. We're going to settle this, Jessie, right here and right now. There's no helicopter to interrupt us this time.'

'And aren't you lucky that chopper turned up when it did? Weren't you afraid you might have a crying female on your hands after you reminded her that there was no room in your life for her back in the real world? Or did you count on me to make things easy for you and give you a great speech about my career and New York City?'

'No room in my life?' He laughed harshly. 'I wasn't

the one who said we had no future together, Jessie. That was your line. There I was, about to tell you I had this great plan—you and I were going to be a team. We'd go into the field together and you'd take pictures while I did text and . . . But you finished that. "I could never live your kind of life," you said . . .'

She tossed her head angrily. 'I didn't say that, cowboy.'

'You sure as hell did, Jessie. You . . .'

'Whatever I said was to make things easier for us both. I thought I owed you that much.'

'Oh, it sounds good, Jessie. If I didn't know better, I'd be tempted to believe you. But the truth is that reality was what you'd been waiting for all along.' He moved closer and lowered his face to hers. 'I broke my tail getting back to you at the hospital in Cheyenne,' he snarled, 'but I needn't have bothered. You didn't even wait to say goodbye, did you? You raced back to New York . . .'

'Broke your tail?' Jessica laughed unpleasantly. 'Sure you did. I cooled my heels for more than four hours . . .'

'I don't suppose you know anything about the Federal Aeronautics Administration, do you, Miss Howard?' Chad asked in an icy voice. 'Do you think meeting with them is like having lunch at the Plaza? Those guys had a million questions and a million papers that had to be filled out. Hell, I ended up walking out on them just because I wanted to get back to you . . .'

'What for? So you could tell me about hyenas?'

'Jackals,' he said furiously, his fingers pressing into the fragile bones in her wrist. 'No, Miss Howard, that's not the reason. Strange as it may seem, I was in a rush to tell you I'd take that damned job at Hunter College so we could be together. I figured if I couldn't talk you into going into the field with me, I'd do it your way. I wanted to tell you I loved you enough so I could do that for us . . .'

Jessica tilted her chin up. 'You didn't have to make any sacrifices for me,' she snapped. 'Before you started that whole speech about your life as a rolling stone, I was going to tell you that Alaska was beginning to sound pretty good.'

'Were you really?' Chad growled.

'Yes, I was,' Jessica snarled. 'But . . .'

Suddenly, they were both silent. Their eyes met in astonishment.

'Jessie?' Chad said softly, 'do you hear what we're saying?'

She took a deep breath. 'I—I hope I do,' she whispered. 'Maybe we should stop arguing for a couple of minutes and sort it out.'

He drew her closer to him. 'Did I hear you say you'd go to Alaska with me, Jessie?'

She nodded. 'That's what I said. And . . . you said you'd live in New York?'

'That's what I said,' he admitted. He smiled and bent his head until their foreheads touched. 'Don't tell me you're speechless, Jessica Howard. That's never happened before.'

She smiled and touched her finger to his moustache. 'I'm trying my best to tell you that I can't accept your offer to live in the city,' she said.

'What?' he said roughly. 'What . . .?'

Jessica laughed softly. 'Temper, temper,' she murmured. 'You see, Corona's offered me a contract. What they want me to do is travel and take pictures. They suggested really remote locations . . .'

'Like Alaska?'

'Like Alaska,' she agreed. 'Like Africa. Like . . . Like wherever you go, Chad, with Corona or without . . .'

'Have you ever been to Boston, Jessie?'

The question was so unexpected that it stopped her cold. She looked at him as if he'd lost his sanity.

'Once,' she said slowly, 'about a year ago. I had a shoot there. But ...'

'Did you like it? I mean, how does it rate on the Howard scale of cities?'

Jessica smiled. 'Better than New York,' she said. 'I know that's heresay, but it's got twice the charm and it's much smaller—and I wish I knew why you were asking me about Boston when I just told you I'd go to Timbuctoo.'

Chad grinned and slipped his arms around her. 'Will Corona hate you for ever if you spend about half of each year in Boston?'

Her eyes widened. 'Chad, what are you talking about?'

'Harvard University is what I'm talking about,' he said with a quick grin. 'Ian Douglas is there now. He read my last paper—hell, it's a long story, but what it comes down to is that they made me an offer I just can't refuse. They want me to teach a graduate seminar every other semester.'

'But ... but I know how you feel about classrooms and campuses ...'

'Jessie,' he said, his eyes gleaming, 'I'm talking about me and a handful of top students, kids who want to study my methods. And the university will fund my field studies with hardly any questions asked. That's not teaching, Jessie, that's passing on knowledge. There's so much to learn about predators ...'

'Like hyenas,' she teased.

Chad nodded. 'Penguins, too,' he said solemnly, and she laughed softly. His hand cupped her face and he looked into her eyes. 'So, what do you think, Miss Howard? Can you survive that kind of existence—half the year in the wilderness and half the year in Boston?'

'Survive it?' she sighed. 'It sounds wonderful. Did you really mean it when you said we could do a book together?'

'Absolutely. A whole series of books. Text and photos by Mr and Mrs Chad O'Bryan. We'll be a terrific team.'

Jessica smiled. 'Not, "Dr and Mrs Chad O'Bryan"?'

Chad shook his head and grinned. 'Too pretentious,' he said.

'I should have figured that,' she laughed. And then she took a deep breath. 'Chad ... I just want you to know that in case you decide you don't really like teaching ...' She smiled at the question in his eyes. 'I'd live anywhere with you, my love,' she said softly. 'In a tent or an igloo or wherever you like. You're what I want—you're all I want.'

His arms tightened around her. 'I love you, Jessie,' he murmured. 'And I have the feeling that seeing a city through your eyes is going to make it seem different. Besides, there are some things only a city can give you.'

'Don't tell me,' she sighed. 'Crime, and pollution, and traffic ...'

He smiled. 'And symphony orchestras, and the theatre, and museums ...'

'And zoos.'

'And zoos,' he agreed. 'And hospitals.'

'Hospitals? Well, yes, but I'm not planning on getting sick ...'

'Neither am I,' he said softly. 'But I thought that's where our children should be born. How does that sound to you?'

'Oh, it sounds wonderful,' she whispered, 'wonderful ...'

'Good,' he said positively, and then a smile flashed across his face. 'Do you realise I'm the man you called a rolling stone just a few minutes ago? Good God, woman, I've got my whole life planned.'

'Are you complaining?' she asked primly.

'The only thing I'm complaining about is that we're wasting time. We've got a lot to do if we're going to leave for Alaska next week. Blood tests and licences and . . .'

'Is there time to fly to Canton? I'd like you to meet my parents. And I'd like to meet your dad and your stepmother, too . . .'

'We'll make time, love. But I can't believe I heard you right. Did you really say you wanted to fly?' Chad teased.

Jessica leaned back in his arms and smiled up at him. 'Definitely, Dr O'Bryan. You see, I spent some time recently with this terrific teacher. I learned some very helpful stuff. He taught me a great way to take my mind off flying . . .'

'Did he really?'

'Um hmm. And he taught me how to cure hypothermia . . .'

He laughed softly. 'Clever man, this teacher of yours.'

Jessica smiled and wound her arms around his neck. 'And he taught me a very important rule of survival. You have to know where you've been, where you are, and where you're going.'

Chad touched his lips to hers and then he smiled. 'That's easy,' he murmured. 'The answer to all three is here, in my arms.'

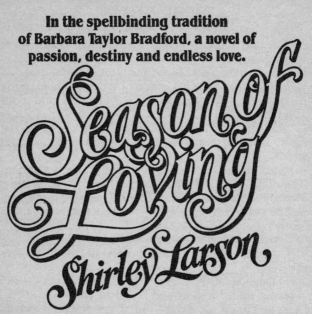

PAMELA BROWNING

...is fireworks on the green at the Fourth of July and prayers said around the Thanksgiving table. It is the dream of freedom realized in thousands of small towns across this great nation.

But mostly, the Heartland is its people. People who care about and help one another. People who cherish traditional values and give to their children the greatest gift, the gift of love.

American Romance presents HEARTLAND, an emotional trilogy about people whose memories, hopes and dreams are bound up in the acres they farm.

HEARTLAND...the story of America.

Don't miss these heartfelt stories: American Romance #237 SIMPLE GIFTS (March), #241 FLY AWAY (April), and #245 HARVEST HOME (May).

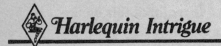

Two exciting new stories each month.

Each title mixes a contemporary, sophisticated romance with the surprising twists and turns of a puzzler... romance with "something more."

Because romance can be quite an adventure.

Romance, Suspense and Adventure